She *should* have been alone

Although disoriented from jet lag and air-sickness pills, Michelle was certain there shouldn't be a man in bed with her.

"I'm a little weak on Emily Post," he said, "but shouldn't we introduce ourselves?" His voice was as warm as his flesh against her bare back.

I'm outta here, she thought wildly, and tugging the sheet around her, she rolled to the side of the bed. When she turned to tell him what she thought of men who accosted unconscious women, her glare was intercepted by the most beautiful eyes. They were incredibly compelling . . . and vaguely familiar.

"You're Alex Lindfors!" she moaned.

"And you are?" he asked politely, amusement twinkling in those eyes.

"Michelle Moens, from Comtron," she mumbled, and when he looked as if she'd struck him, she added, "Who did you *think* I was?"

All traces of laughter gone from his face, Alex replied, "I thought you were my birthday present. . . ."

Sarah Hawkes hasn't always written books, but they've certainly been the focus of her life. Always an avid reader of Harlequin romances, Sally harbored a secret desire to write them even as she advanced in her career as a librarian, following opportunities from Philadelphia, to Illinois and finally to Arkansas. It was only after settling in Little Rock where, she says, an abundance of romance writers live, that Sally pursued her own writing. The result is *An Unmarried Man,* her first Harlequin Temptation and a book that reflects Sally's love of romantic comedy.

An Unmarried Man
SARAH HAWKES

Harlequin Books

TORONTO • NEW YORK • LONDON
AMSTERDAM • PARIS • SYDNEY • HAMBURG
STOCKHOLM • ATHENS • TOKYO • MILAN

FORTY YEARS OF
Romance

Published August 1989

ISBN 0-373-25364-8

1

"THIS IS VERY PLEASANT, sweetheart, but shouldn't you tell me your name first?"

Michelle Moens froze, the unmistakably amused—and indulgent—male voice stopping her from snuggling into the covers. She kept her eyes squeezed shut, even though the strong light against her eyelids told her it was morning. Unfortunately she had two problems. One, she didn't remember where she was, and two, although disoriented, she was certain there shouldn't be a man in her bed with her.

She decided to take one problem at a time. Her usually analytical mind was sluggish from jet lag and two prescription pills for air sickness, as was her body. Her month of traveling was catching up to her with a vengeance. She recited the names of the cities on her itinerary: Shreveport, Beaumont, Longview and Dallas. Then finally Chicago, for a routine check of Lindfors House Limited's software.

Chicago, at the Lindfors House corporate apartment—that's where she was. She remembered the intimidating manservant who had let her in and directed her to the bedroom, apologizing for not having had her room ready. Almost asleep on her feet, she'd stripped and fallen into bed without even bothering to braid her waist-length, strawberry-blond hair.

She'd gotten into bed alone, she knew, which brought her swiftly back to problem number two. Opening her brown eyes cautiously, she hoped the deep, amused voice had been a dream. But there was another body in the bed, a masculine body. A body she was in embarrassing proximity to, her breasts pressed intimately against his torso. Her view was limited to his tanned chest, liberally covered with golden hairs, and the rumpled slate-gray sheets beyond.

"I'm a little weak on Emily Post, but I think we really should introduce ourselves," he said politely, his voice rumbling in her ears. "Ladies first, I think."

While he spoke in an unthreatening manner, he gently stroked her bare back beneath her curtain of hair. Michelle stiffened at the intimate touch. *That's it,* she decided, no real plan in mind. *I'm outta here.*

Her primary thought was escape as she tugged the sheet around her and rolled over the side of the bed. Unfortunately her lethargic body didn't cooperate, and she landed on her backside in an inelegant heap. Her only consolation was that now she was decently covered.

"Hey, are you all right, honey?" the man inquired from just above her head, his amusement replaced by concern.

She leaned back on one elbow, brushing her hair out of her face so she could see. Anger and mortification warred within her as she raised her head to tell him what she thought of men who accosted unconscious women. At least, that had been her intention.

Her glare was intercepted by the most beautiful eyes she had ever seen in a man—deep ultramarine, and framed by ridiculously thick gold-tipped lashes.

Amusement still lurked in their depths, highlighting the flecks of lighter blue in the irises. His wasn't a handsome face, his aggressive jaw and prominent nose contrasting strangely with his stunning eyes. However, the combination was compelling . . . and vaguely familiar.

"Do I pass inspection?" His deep, rich voice drew her bemused attention to his mouth, which somehow didn't match his rugged Viking bone structure. The outline of the upper lip was delicately defined above the squared, sensual thrust of his full bottom lip. He smiled with practised charm, a solitary dimple appearing in his left cheek.

"You're Alec Lindfors," she moaned with a flash of recognition. Her first instinct was to pull the sheet over her face, which she knew was now flushed with color. This was the president of the import company where she'd be working.

"And you are?" he returned, propping his head up with his hand as he settled his elbow on the mattress.

She ducked her head and mumbled the words reluctantly. "Michelle Moens from Comtron."

With that she succeeded in wiping the last trace of laughter from his face. In fact, he looked as if she had struck him. "Who did you *think* I was?" she asked.

"My birthday present."

"What?" Her alto voice rose to a high pitch. Through her astonishment she wondered if she'd hit her head when she dropped off the bed.

"Well, what would you think if you woke up and found a nude woman in your arms on your thirty-eighth birthday?" he asked, as if they were having a perfectly rational conversation.

Michelle blinked at him, then shook her head, her lips pursed in answer to his preposterous question. She knew it was time to take control and stop this strange discussion before she got a permanent crick in her neck. Placing her hand firmly on the hem of the sheet to secure it against her collarbone, she moved to get up. Lying on the floor with Alec Lindfors leaning over her was not a power position.

Immediately she regretted her precipitate action. She'd managed to pin her hair to the floor when she'd put weight on her hand to push herself upright. A surreptitious glance at the bed showed her that her companion was watching her with avid interest.

Her second attempt was successful. Once on her feet, she flashed a smug, somewhat triumphant smile at her audience, tossing one corner of the sheet over her shoulder with a flourish. Her bravado was short-lived, however, because Alec Lindfors hadn't moved a muscle. He was stretched out in front of her, gloriously, unabashedly, naked. Michelle spun around, emitting a squeak, her hair swirling over her bare shoulders in a curtain of red-gold. Too late she snapped her eyes shut in embarrassment. Adding to her disquiet, her traitorous mind taunted her with the fact that Alec was a very virile candidate for a centerfold.

"I think we'll continue this discussion more suitably dressed and reinforced by some good, strong coffee. This certainly isn't Molloy's idea of dressing for success." Alec's voice was tinged with regret as he ran an appreciative eye over Michelle. "Now don't peek."

He saw a lovely rose-color flush tint her flawless ivory skin, and wondered why he was behaving so chivalrously. A woman with the most enticing pair of

chocolate-brown eyes he'd ever seen was standing,
nearly naked, within arm's reach. The gossipmongers
of the press would have a field day with the situation.
He shrugged and got to his feet before he gave in to his
baser instincts and demanded possession of his sheet.

As he padded across the thick rust-colored carpet to
the closet, he wondered how to explain himself to the
unflappable Glynn. Or better yet, what his taciturn
manservant would have to say about this little fiasco.
Shrugging into his velour robe and quickly selecting
fresh clothing, he admitted Glynn hadn't known Alec
had come back into the city yesterday to play soccer,
instead of staying home in Lake Forest until Monday
morning as usual. And Ms Moens wasn't expected until tomorrow, so Glynn probably hadn't had the guest
room made up and simply put her in this room last
night. Alec hadn't anticipated staying in town himself;
however, when his teammates discovered that it was his
birthday, there was no stopping the celebration.

It was past midnight when he'd decided to head
home. Hours of rigorous play and serious beer drinking combined to make the perfect tranquilizer. He'd
fallen asleep the moment he'd stripped off his clothes
and crawled into bed, completely unaware of the cur-
vaceous figure next to him until he'd awoken to find her
in his arms in the morning.

"All right, I'm decent," he announced. Eyeing the
abundant fall of reddish gold hair that cloaked Michelle's body, he let out a breath of regret. He ruthlessly dismissed the memory of her lush breasts pressing
against his chest, as he turned and swiftly left the room
before he gave in to the desire to return to bed. A cold
shower in the guest room would have to suffice.

Michelle moaned in despair over her own stupidity the moment he was gone. Awkwardly she waddled to the bed and sat down. She was a competent business-woman with a reputation for staying cool and calm in a crisis. This morning she'd acted with all the finesse of a teenybopper, instead of a woman who'd risen swiftly in responsibility at Comtron over the past three years. Male voices filtering through the inch-wide opening in the door interrupted her thoughts and made her very conscious of the need to dress.

She groped at the end of the bed for her suitcase. Flinging the larger of her two bags onto the oak-framed bed with one hand, she grabbed the first article of clothing packed inside. When she was safely covered by the silky nightshirt, she headed for the shower.

The warm water didn't have the soothing effect she'd anticipated. Instead it brought back the disturbing memory of Alec Lindfors's warm skin next to hers. He certainly lived up to his reputation, she reflected grimly. She could now believe the myriad newspaper accounts that had accompanied his company's profile, despite what she knew from his younger sister.

Michelle was thoughtful as she got dressed, then coiled her long hair at the crown of her head. She wished she'd paid closer attention to Jessica's prattle about her brother. At college, Jessica's rambling had masked her concern while her brother was in Vietnam, then convalescing in a VA hospital. Now, years later, she joked about his purported exploits with the ladies in her letters or on the phone.

When Michelle had been assigned the Lindfors job, she hadn't felt it necessary to mention her friendship with Jessica. After this morning's lunacy, she definitely wouldn't bring it up. Alec wouldn't connect Michelle Henrietta Moens with Jessica's shy roommate "Hal."

Dismissing all thoughts of her college days, she tended to the more serious business of checking her appearance before facing that man again. Her navy slacks and blue print blouse seemed respectable enough. She set her jaw as she headed for the door, determined that Alec Lindfors meet the businesswoman Michelle Moens, not his recent bedmate.

THE LIVING ROOM was dominated by an entire wall of windows that had been concealed by drawn curtains the previous night. Absorbed in the view, she barely noticed the stark design of the Scandinavian-style furnishings as she crossed the room. The city of Chicago seemed to be spread at her feet. She identified such familiar landmarks as the Sears Building and the Marina Towers, which had been part of a spectacular geometric display of lights when she'd flown over the night before.

"It's even more impressive at night," Alec commented directly behind her, as if he'd read her thoughts.

She stiffened and turned swiftly to face her host. He'd showered and changed into a charcoal-gray pin-striped suit and a cobalt-blue shirt. Michelle regarded the debonair man who stood before her, his jacket slung casually over his shoulder, and decided he knew full well his clothing accentuated his golden tan and the platinum streaks in his hair. In fact, she thought with resentment, he looked too darn good to be true.

Alec, too, was looking over his recent bed partner. Although he regretted that her hair was no longer down, the soft halo of reddish amber complimented her heart-shaped face. Now, he decided, she would be a perfect subject for a Sargent portrait, the epitome of an Edwardian society lady.

Her creamy skin was flawless, the sprinkling of freckles across her nose, which he'd found so appealing, now artfully concealed. He knew he could lose himself for hours in the velvet-brown of her eyes, and her incredibly kissable mouth.... Alec wanted to taste those pouting, bow lips in the worst way.

A very tempting package, indeed, he thought with regret. His eyes trailed down her rounded figure, appreciating each delightful curve that had pressed against him just half an hour earlier. He guessed she was about five-foot-four—perfect next to his own six feet.

Reluctantly his glance returned to her face, and he knew he was in trouble. Her sable brows were raised, her mouth pursed in irritation at his indolent inspection. Quickly he motioned her toward the dining area. Watching the delicious sway of her hips, he could not hold back another sigh of longing. When he seated her at the planked pine table, the determined tilt of her chin told him he needed to mask his thoughts.

"Well, it looks as though Glynn is more prepared this morning. He was very sorry he inconvenienced you by not having your room ready last night," Alec remarked as he unwound his intricately folded linen napkin. Silently he finished, *and the old boy is certainly pulling out all the stops to make up for it.* He dug into a perfectly prepared grapefruit that nested in a bed of chipped ice.

Michelle's only answer was a slight nod, and the silence continued while they ate their fruit. Both, however, surreptitiously glanced at each other through lowered lashes.

Michelle was relieved Alec had seated her facing the windows. When she finished her grapefruit, she was able to study him while appearing to enjoy the view. She supposed that with his reputation, handling the morning after was routine. It was the morning after what that plagued her. She had a strange memory of a beach shrouded in pink mist, and the disturbing feeling that she knew what it was like to kiss Alec Lindfors.

"Regretfully nothing happened. So you can stop staring so fiercely at the skyline."

Her gaze flew to his cocky grin. Damn the man, he was reading her mind again. Well, he was mistaken if he thought he could embarrass her. She plotted vengefully as the stout Glynn removed their used dishes and served delectable-looking omelets. The minute he left the room she aimed a deceptively innocent smile at her host.

"Are you a natural blond?" she asked. "Your hair's not light all over."

The sound of a dish shattering in the kitchen accompanied Alec's choking cough as he swallowed his first bite of a seasoned egg with difficulty. Michelle's guileless smile remained firm, her carefully widened eyes never wavering from the narrowed, blue-eyed stare of Alec Lindfors.

After an endless moment he relaxed, a reluctant smile appearing to show his dimple. "Direct hit, Ms Moens. Yes, I am. I've always been a two-toned blond. Now at the advanced age of thirty-eight there is more white than blond. All Lindfors men have had blond hair, while the women tend toward brown hair that never grays. Satisfied?"

"Yes, thank you," she replied demurely, turning her attention to her plate. She was afraid he would read her knowledge of one particular brunette Lindfors woman.

After a moment his expression changed and became serious. "We could forget this morning and last night ever happened. Pretend we just met over the breakfast table. Agreed?"

She blinked owlishly for a minute, then realized he was in earnest. There was still a small doubt in the back of her mind, but she nodded her agreement.

"So how do you plan to spend your day?"

Michelle valiantly swallowed her first response. By admitting a desire to return to bed she would only put herself back on thin ice. "I thought I'd walk down to the Art Institute to visit my favorite impressionists and be envious of the Thorne miniature furniture exhibit, unless you'd rather I started working today?"

"No, take the day to recharge as you'd planned. Since you've been to Chicago before, you can pick the restaurant for dinner. Where are we going?"

She blurted out the name of her favorite German restaurant without thinking. "Now wait a minute. I didn't say I was going out to dinner with you."

The efficient Glynn appeared to help his employer into his suit jacket. "Tut, tut. Remember, it's my birthday. Glynn will get your things settled in the guest room while you're out sight-seeing."

Michelle was fuming that he had the nerve to treat her as a bimbo. So much for their truce. Jumping to her feet and throwing her napkin down on the table, she said, "Now just a damn minute, Mr. Lindfors."

He turned with a disturbing grace, casually tossing his keys in one hand. "Glynn will drive you to the Art Institute or on any other errands you have today. I wouldn't want you too tired to enjoy our evening."

She stalked around the table to confront him, but he wasn't finished with her quite yet. "By the way, is your birthmark shaped like a butterfly or a daisy?"

Michelle came to an abrupt stop and shot him a fierce frown. Mustering as much dignity as she could, she turned and walked stiffly to the bedroom. She wasn't about to let him witness her blushing again; he'd had enough entertainment at her expense for the morning.

Just as she slammed the bedroom door she heard him call out again.

"Don't forget—six o'clock sharp for dinner."

She stormed over to the bedroom window and stared sightlessly out at the city, ignoring the bed beside her. How had he seen that birthmark? It was low on her back, next to the only dimples she possessed. As the obvious answer came to her, so did understanding of Alec's most recent tactic: he was trying to keep her off balance. But he wouldn't succeed.

"We can forget this morning ever happened," she mimicked, and swept up her navy battle jacket and purse. She was one lady Alec Lindfors would discover had a mind of her own. She figured Glynn would be occupied clearing away the breakfast dishes, so she could tiptoe out of the apartment to spend the day exactly as she'd planned. Mr. Condescending Lindfors could take his suggestions and shove them in his briefcase.

ALEC WHISTLED HAPPILY as he waited for the elevator to arrive. He was more than satisfied with his recent victory. Ms Michelle Moens was an interesting proposition. His mind still retained the alluring image of her face flushed in anger, her eyes sparkling in rage.

His mood was matched by the brilliant spring sunshine as he strolled south on Michigan Avenue minutes later. The satisfied grin that relaxed his craggy features even drew the momentary interest of some of the rush-hour pedestrians. But when Alec's thoughts turned to the real reason Michelle had come to Chicago, a frown replaced his cheerful grin. That infernal computer. Although his company had requested the visit from a Comtron representative a few months ago, no one had suspected how badly help would be needed. Help that had to be confidential and handled subtly. His antics this morning might have just destroyed the possibility of any cooperation on Michelle Moens's part.

He already knew he was walking a narrow line between business and pleasure. From now on he would have to tread more carefully. As he continued the few short blocks to his office, he was disturbed that pleasure kept coming out ahead of business in his thoughts.

WHEN MICHELLE RETURNED to the apartment late in the afternoon, she was tired, but refreshed in spirit. Glynn greeted her with his usual unreadable expression. Her profuse thank-yous for his meticulous unpacking of her belongings were somewhat overdone because her conscience was bothering her; it wasn't Glynn's fault he worked for an arrogant lech.

She grimaced at the tasteful pine furniture in her new room. After hours of gazing enviously at the exquisite, miniature reproductions of the Thorne collection, modern furniture held little appeal. Everything seemed either square or flat. She assumed that most of Alec's possessions, including the Danish-modern bedroom suite in his room, probably came from his import company's warehouse.

The thought of Lindfors House led her to look for her burgundy briefcase. She needed to prepare herself for tomorrow's meeting. Alec wouldn't intimidate her when it came to work, the one area in which she'd never experienced failure. An hour later she snapped her notebook shut where it rested on her knees, leaned back against the square headboard and thoughtfully chewed on the stem of her reading glasses.

There was something wrong with Lindfors's request for new security measures. His current program should suit his needs, but he was apparently not satisfied. Granted he did need an upgrade to support the expansion of his new mail-order business— A discreet tap on the door interrupted her calculations.

Glynn stood in the doorway. "Excuse me, miss, but I took the liberty of doing your laundry."

Michelle sat up abruptly, gaping at the sight of her delicate French lingerie in his blunt hands. Quelling her amusement, she pointed wordlessly to the dresser.

"Have you worked for Mr. Lindfors a long time, Glynn?" she asked. Moving to sit cross-legged on the bed, she rested her chin in one hand as he handled her intimate apparel with care. No one had ever waited on her hand and foot this way.

"About fifteen years, miss," he returned politely.

She noted that his clothing suited the image of the well-turned-out butler. A spotless, starched white shirt, faultlessly creased black trousers and a military striped tie were protected by a gray apron. His face, though, could stop a clock.

"Where did you meet?" she continued, growing curious about this contradictory man.

"In Tokyo, miss," he murmured as he carefully shut the top drawer. "Have you decided what to wear this evening? Shall I freshen it?"

"Er, yes, the navy sheath on the left." She slapped her hand over her mouth to stifle a giggle as Glynn turned to retrieve the dress. She felt as if she'd stepped into a British mystery set on a country estate—except the butler was from Brooklyn.

"Is there anything else?"

"Yes, the jacket is next to the dress." There was a sudden silence. Casually she turned her head, and an involuntary smile formed. Glynn was holding out the cocoon-style jacket with his thumb and forefinger, clearly unable to make head or tail of it. "A gentle steam should set it to rights, don't you think, Glynn?"

"Just so, Miss Hal," he answered with aplomb, a twinkle in his eyes as he took in her shocked expression. With an almost imperceptible wink, he left the room.

Michelle stared at the closed door. The man was unbelievable—he could read her mind as easily as his employer. She was sure Alec had no idea she was Jessica's old roommate. He would have used that information this morning if he'd made the connection.

But how had Glynn known? The code of masculine nicknames had been devised in college. Jessica had become "Fred," from her middle name, Wilfreda, a name almost as appalling, Michelle thought, as her own

Henrietta. Olivia and Patrice Rafaela, their two other roommates, had become "Noll" and "Rafe."

She knew it wasn't earth-shattering that Glynn knew, but she didn't want her personal life under examination. Her being qualified for the Lindfors House job was the result of hard work and experience. More disturbing was the thought that Alec could discover she was Jessica's wallflower roommate from college, and she didn't want pity or sympathy, especially from a man who had women panting in line. Pity was something she'd become all too familiar with not so long ago, thanks to another libidinous male.

Glynn was keeping the information to himself for now and seemed amused by it. Well, she would just have to wait and see when—or if—he decided to squeal on her. She didn't want to question him, which might give the secret too much importance. For now she'd worry about her computer work and play a waiting game with the amused manservant.

ALEC GLADLY ACCEPTED the squat glass of bourbon on the rocks from Glynn as he waited for Michelle to join him for dinner. He knew he was unreasonably nervous and anxious about seeing her again, but what bothered him most was why. Why a woman he'd met only hours earlier had been uppermost in his mind all day. He wasn't sure he was on edge from anticipation or the chance that he'd be disappointed.

His usual total immersion in his work had been impossible today. His thoughts continually wandered, bringing him back again and again to the delightful memory of Michelle's shapely body in his arms. Simply by closing his eyes he could recall their naked bodies blanketed by her thick curtain of red-gold hair. Abruptly he took a healthy swig of his drink, hoping the cold liquor would cool his sudden surge of hot desire.

This is ridiculous! The chastisement was compounded by Glynn's amused expression while he puttered behind the bar. *He knows I changed clothes three times,* Alec thought disgustedly, *and that I'm behaving like an idiot with overactive hormones.*

Just then he heard the sound of the guest room doorknob turning. His heart jumped and his pulse rate accelerated as, from the corner of his eye, he watched the door slowly open. Quickly he looked around for something, anything, on which to focus.

A blank space among the pictures dotting the wall behind the bar captured his searching glance. He concentrated on what was supposed to be there and why it was missing.

"What happened to Jess's college picture, Glynn?" He almost sagged in relief that his voice came out at his normal, low pitch. As he gestured at the blank space with his glass, he could see Michelle moving toward him. Even in his peripheral vision, she looked lovelier than he remembered.

"It slipped while I was dusting this morning and the glass broke. I've sent it out to be repaired," Glynn responded shortly, pointedly gazing to Alec's left as he spoke.

Alec was relieved that the picture wasn't damaged. Jess and her little pigtailed friend in the photograph had helped him through some hard times, and he regarded it as a talisman of sorts. However, the faded fourteen-year-old picture was quickly forgotten when he finally turned to face Michelle.

"Ah, Michelle, you're very punctual," he managed with forced cheerfulness, running a discerning eye over her luscious figure. He valiantly ignored his first impulse to take her in his arms. Instead he thrust his half-empty glass at Glynn and stepped forward to take Michelle's arm. Now he knew what he had been feeling. Anxiety that she would stand him up for dinner after his high-handed tactics that morning.

"Don't wait up, Glynn," he called out with a dismissive wave as he ushered Michelle toward the front door. He didn't notice Glynn winking at his companion.

2

THE EVENING TURNED OUT to be surprisingly pleasant and uneventful much to Michelle's relief. Alec acted as if she were any other business associate, and she relaxed, forgetting, under the influence of superb food and service, her earlier unease.

"You're an interesting person, Michelle," Alec remarked as they entered his apartment later in the evening.

"Oh, really? Why is that?" she asked absently, her attention drawn immediately to the living-room windows. She shrugged off her jacket, entranced by the lights of the city.

Alec went to the bar, removed his blazer and tie, then rolled up his sleeves and began pouring them each a cognac. "Interesting because I don't know many women who request German food and then order bock beer with it." He walked to her side carrying two lead-glass snifters.

"After weeks of Tex-Mex and Creole, I needed something a little more subtle, though not bland," she explained as she rotated her glass, watching the movement of the golden liquor. Beneath lowered lashes she pretended to study her drink, aware of Alec's tanned forearms and muscular chest, partially revealed by three loosened buttons.

"When was the last time you ate at home?" he continued, pursuing their first personal conversation of the night. Dinner had covered general talk about books, arts, films and the theater; now he was curious about the woman who'd accidentally shared his bed.

Actually, "curious" was an understatement, he thought as his eyes ran over her lovely profile and smooth shoulders, bare except for the two wide straps that held up her dress. He did not allow his gaze to linger too long on the tempting swell of her breasts. She fascinated him and still he didn't know why. Perhaps it was the intriguing way they'd met. However, it wasn't just the memory of her soft body in his arms. There was something about the lady—her animated conversation, the way she used her hands to talk . . . any number of things. He hadn't pinned down her special, elusive quality, but he would.

"Home? I'm beginning to think there is no such place." She sighed, thinking wistfully of her condo in Atlanta. Disturbed by his intense look, she moved to the couch that faced the windows and settled herself securely in a corner, one leg tucked under the other. "Except for two overnight visits, I haven't been there in one month and twelve days—or five cities, however you want to count it."

"No wonder you were confused when you arrived." He nodded thoughtfully as he joined her, unaware his words had caused her to start. "Tomorrow night it's Glynn's broiled trout."

She groaned appreciatively, as expected, but her mind was no longer on food. Watching him out of the corner of her eye, she was not deceived when he casually draped his arm over the back of the leather couch.

His expression had turned speculative since their return. Half his shirt gaped open, revealing the mat of golden hair that she knew arrowed down his chest. She suppressed a shiver as she remembered the soft texture against her skin; it was a dangerous memory. She was going to remain a safe distance from this man, even if part of her did respond to his masculinity. Perhaps rather than laughing with her, Glynn's amusement earlier had been directed at her as Alec's next victim.

"Shall I freshen your drink?" Alec's deep voice broke into her disturbing thoughts.

"No, thanks. I need to get to sleep soon to be alert for tomorrow," she answered, thrusting her empty glass at him but carefully avoiding any contact with his fingers. "Just one more look at the view and then I'm off."

She stood and went to the window. As she studied the night skyline she attempted to forget her host, focusing only on the lights, until his warm hands clasped her bare shoulders.

"I can see you'll be easy to entertain," he said softly into her ear, his breath disturbing the curls at her neck. "You'll be happy with a few excursions to the top of the Sears Tower."

She laughed nervously to hide her reaction to his touch. "I expect no less than dinner at the Ninety-fifth."

His deep laughter skated down her spine as he turned her still figure to face him. Tiny points of fire sparked within her as his arms moved to entrap her. She stared mutely into eyes that now mirrored a disquieting emotion.

Mesmerized, she offered no resistance as he lowered his head. His sculpted mouth brushed lightly over hers, the teasing pressure parting her soft lips. This accomplished, he deepened the kiss. Her half-conscious experience of the previous night did not prepare her for the electric thrill that raced through her. Without conscious thought she ran her hands up his arms to link them around his neck.

Searching hands pulled her hips against the hard thrust of his body. A small sound of gratification started in her throat as his tongue delved into the moist interior of her mouth. She moved restlessly against his firm body to assuage the desire that had begun to smoulder deep within her. When it seemed as if he would draw back, she reached up to trap his head between her hands, feathering her fingers into his thick hair. She grew bolder, caressing the side of his head alternately with her palm and the back of her hand as Alec crushed her against him.

"You're incredible," he whispered hoarsely as he abandoned her lips for the wildly beating pulse at the base of her throat. "I thought I'd dreamed you tasted like cherries this morning. Now it's brandied cherries."

"Lip gloss," she murmured absently, kneading his shoulders. No man had ever made her feel this way. It was not the lingering effects of her erotic dream, as she had rationalized; it was the man himself.

"No, sweetheart, you are unique," he argued softly, following the column of her throat to nibble on her earlobe. He wanted more of her. Alec slid his hand up the soft curve of her waist to rest at the side of her breast. "I've never known another woman who could make me this crazy with a kiss."

His reassurances set off an inner alarm in the back of Michelle's mind. The excitement he had kindled so quickly died at the careless phrase. She moved her seductive hands, which had been caressing his back, to his waist. Surprise more than strength allowed her to push him away.

"If you try a few more women, maybe you'll get lucky again, Mr. Lindfors," she snapped, moving quickly to maintain the distance between them. She grabbed her jacket and purse before striding toward her room. A thought struck when she was halfway across the room, and she pivoted abruptly to face him. "Or better yet, pay a visit to your wife."

Pensively he watched her turn and stomp into the guest room. When she slammed the door he murmured, "Happy birthday, Alec."

On the other side of the closed door Michelle leaned against the smooth wood to steady her anger. Anger directed at her own foolishness. She knew that men, especially married men, had few scruples when it came to their sex drives. This time she would not be the other woman. Alec Lindfors would have to find another playmate, since he wasn't content with his estranged wife.

Still fuming, she stripped off her clothes and considered telling Glynn to burn the small heap she left in the middle of the floor. She'd like to do the same to an effigy of his boss. She removed her makeup with vicious swipes of the washcloth, then punished her teeth and gums with her toothbrush and braided her hair with jerky movements.

She was still agitated when she returned to the bedroom, yanked open dresser drawers and slammed them shut as she searched for her nightgown. The sight of herself in the cheval mirror as she stepped out of her peach teddy halted her movements. Putting her thumbs in her ears, she wiggled her fingers at the hour-glass shape she saw reflected. All the polite terms came to mind—pear shaped, figure eight, full figured—then they degenerated to pleasantly plump, hippy, chubby.

"Not to forget Happy, Sneezy and Grumpy," she muttered under her breath while she slipped on her ice-green nightshirt. "They were overweight dwarfs, too."

With a weary sigh she did a belly flop onto the bed. Her chin propped in her hand, she thought wistfully of her mother's tall, rail-thin silhouette and her sister Irene's beauty-queen figure. Then she had an image of her three closest friends. Jessica and Patrice were over five inches taller than she. The tops of their thighs were even with her waist, for pete's sake. Olivia was about her height but fifteen pounds lighter. They could all eat like lumberjacks without counting a single calorie or carbohydrate. However, she could stand next to anything remotely fattening and gain five pounds. None of them had been called "Pudge" as a child. Unlike Irene, who was accomplished at everything, her only talents were thinking and eating.

From the pictures she'd seen, Alec Lindfors's lady friends seemed to be anorexics rather than calorie counters. He must be between women to make a pass at her, she decided. Over the past month she'd gained five pounds eating restaurant food and not exercising as usual.

"Sit-ups, leg lifts and fanny crawl tomorrow morning," she muttered resignedly as she stretched to reach her silver-tone travel alarm. Mentally she crossed off her favorite restaurant at Water Tower Place, ruthlessly deleting cream of broccoli soup, crusty French bread and a cherry croissant from her taste buds' memory.

Tomorrow Alec Lindfors would be confronted with a more persevering Michelle Moens. He would see her ability as a businesswoman, where her real talent lay. From now on she'd act differently, she determined as she flipped off the light and settled on her back. Another married man was not going to make a patsy out of her, especially when she knew in advance that this one was married.

The memories of Stuart's lies stiffened her resolve. She turned to an exercise Patrice had taught her in college. Clearing her mind of everything, she gradually relaxed each part of her body. In a trancelike state, she repeated one thought: no matter how attractive, a married man had no part in her life.

IT WAS AMAZING how empty his bed seemed tonight, Alec reflected, staring up at the ceiling. He didn't need to look at his digital clock to know he'd lain awake for two and a half hours. Two and a half hours that he'd spent remembering and analyzing every encounter with the cause of his insomnia—Michelle. Her image refused to be dismissed from his thoughts.

At first he'd decided the angry lady wasn't his type. Then he admitted he didn't have a specific type. He dated an equal number of blondes, brunettes and redheads of varying heights and builds. The common ground seemed to be that all were career women, intelligent, personable, charming and in no need of a commitment. He did restrict the age difference to ten years, but he wasn't certain of Michelle's age. She could be anywhere from mid-twenties to his sister's early thirties.

He kept returning to the one disturbing difference. Michelle was the first woman to spend an entire night in his bed, albeit a platonic one for the most part. He never brought his bed companions to his home, either in the city or to the house in Lake Forest. He wanted few entanglements with his pleasures. Any lovemaking took place at the lady's home and he never spent the night or felt tempted to stay. Now his established pattern was broken, and this disturbed him. For the first time he actually regretted his little game in fooling the newspapers. Maybe he shouldn't have let their sordid fantasies about his personal life go unchecked.

But his real disquiet stemmed from the fact he was taking a good look at himself, and he didn't like what he saw—a very selfish man with little concern for anyone's feelings but his own, if he still had any. The only women he allowed close to him were his sweet, scatterbrained mother and his slightly crazy sister; the others were simply a diversion from work. All his energies were channeled into his father's business.

Now he was haunted by one woman who filled his thoughts and senses after knowing her just a single day. In twenty-four hours his emotions were twisted into knots. While Michelle lay contentedly sleeping in his guest room, he wasn't even able to relax. A simple turn of his head toward the pillow she'd used brought an enticing whiff of her elusive perfume. The smell of roses and the other mysterious flower invaded his memory, causing his body to respond automatically.

Disgusted with his lack of control, Alec flung back the covers and stood. Ruthlessly he stripped off the

sheets and both pillowcases, hurling them across the
room with a curse and not caring what Glynn would
think. For good measure he dropped to the floor and
pumped his rebellious body into control with push-ups.
On the ninetieth extension of his straining arms, he decided Michelle Moens would not have him at her mercy
any longer. He crawled onto the bare mattress with a
smile of grim satisfaction, despite his labored breathing and accelerated heartbeat.

MICHELLE WANTED TO TAKE her briefcase and slam it
into Alec Lindfors's shins as she trotted down the busy
sidewalk three steps behind him. Like his sister, he had
a long stride that, being six inches shorter and in a
straight skirt, Michelle couldn't match. Suspiciously
she wondered if he really did walk to work each day.
Then she was distracted by yet another business-
woman attired in a suit strangely accessorized with
smudged track shoes. That made her tally an even
dozen on their trek down Michigan and Wacker ave-
nues.

"Isn't it invigorating walking along the river in the
morning?" Alec called back over his shoulder as Michelle dodged another pedestrian. He'd finally been
forced to stop by a red light and heavy traffic.

A train passing overhead on the el track allowed Michelle to catch her breath. With great restraint she kept
from sticking out her tongue at Alec's complacent
smile. Occupied with keeping up and simulating normal breathing, she didn't have time to appreciate the
scenery. Now, after barely speaking five words this
morning, he wanted to be sociable.

"What's that building?" she inquired after they crossed the street. The stone building in question seemed dwarfed among the towering skyscrapers. Its aged facade, however, was at home among the concrete balustrades and tarnished lampposts they passed on their side of the Chicago River.

"Hmm? Oh, that's the Merchandise Mart," he answered, sounding preoccupied. "It's a good landmark to remember, since my office is just a few more blocks."

She gritted her teeth to suppress a groan. "This is so pleasant. Comtron is out of the city, so I'm used to driving to work. You miss so awfully much from a car, and I've always depended on taxis when I've been here before."

Alec nodded absently in response to her dripping sweet Georgia-peach words, but remained silent for the rest of their walk. Michelle allowed herself a tiny, satisfied smile. She assumed she'd managed to pass some sort of test. As they entered the elevator for the final leg of the trip she made a mental note to buy track shoes for their daily hike.

In the crowded elevator Alec maintained his silence, which she chose to interpret as sulking. He stalked down the carpeted hallway and stopped abruptly at a double wooden door that bore the Lindfors House yellow-and-blue logo. Thrusting open the right-hand door, he motioned her into the reception area.

"Katrin, this is Ms Moens from Comtron. She'll be here checking our computer," Alec said pleasantly to the well-groomed brunette behind the desk. "Michelle, this is Katrin Holtz, our receptionist."

"How do you do, Ms Holtz." Michelle automatically extended her hand. She noticed the quick, side-long look the woman gave her boss.

"'Katrin,' please, Ms Moans," the dark-haired woman returned with a reserved smile that did not reach her eyes, as she shook Michelle's hand.

"Thank you and please, call me 'Michelle.' I'm used to an informal office." She didn't bother to correct Katrin's mispronunciation of her name. There was something not quite right with the woman's response. She couldn't pinpoint what it was, so she avoided compounding any problems.

"Katrin, I'll be taking Michelle around the sections if Britt needs me," Alec said as he cupped Michelle's elbow, urging her through the doorway into the main office.

Michelle tried not to stiffen at his touch, and she smiled tentatively at Katrin's nod of farewell. When she turned her full attention back to the man next to her, she became uncomfortably aware of the effect his sudden proximity had on her. The warmth of his hand through the sleeve of her tan twill jacket seemed to travel swiftly up her arm and through her entire body. The tantalizing smell of his spicy after-shave reminded her too clearly of their first morning together, in his bed.

"I'll take you through each department first and let you meet the supervisors," Alec said. "We'll end up in the computer room."

"Fine," she answered softly, hoping the response didn't sound as inadequate to his ears. She knew it was ridiculous to think he could really read her thoughts. However, she stepped away from his courteous hold at the first opportunity. Silently she recited her resolve of the previous night like a mantra. Combined with the visual reinforcement of Alec, fully clothed in his brown three-piece suit, it helped dispel—somewhat—the memory of his muscular body lying next to hers.

Soon there was another, more serious distraction. The same underlying coolness that she'd noticed in Katrin was present with each introduction to the department supervisors. She knew meeting new people was usually awkward, but this was extreme. The men and women would smile and exchange greetings, but the pleasantness was only on the surface. After a half-dozen frosty greetings, Michelle was beginning to respond in the same manner. She gritted her teeth to tolerate each mangling of her last name, which only increased her inner tension. She started noticeably when Alec stopped at the end of the hallway before the door labeled Computer Room, Keep Closed, and, instead of opening the door as she'd expected, turned toward her.

Her gaze flew to his face to encounter his piercing blue gaze. His expression was no longer distracted or impersonal. The seemingly leering smile made her want to step back, but she stood her ground. Alec was again the man she had innocently slept with. She waited uneasily for him to speak. A tingling feeling that she dared not analyze coursed through her.

"You know, you might consider changing your name to 'Moans' legally, since it's so suitable." The amusement in his expression contradicted his conversational tone. She didn't respond. Straightening her spine, she raised her eyebrows in mild inquiry as her chin came up.

His smile widened as he braced his hand on the doorknob and leaned casually against the jamb. "It reminds me of those delightful little sounds you make when I kiss you."

Michelle could feel the heated flush begin beneath the open toes of her brown pumps and travel swiftly upward to her hairline. She looked everywhere but at the man blocking the door. Although she wasn't sure of Alec's intent, she never had responded well to flattery. Compliments to a once-overweight adolescent—who was still overly conscious of every centimeter of her body—were accepted with wary discomfort. While secure in business matters, her personal life was constantly haunted by the ghost of her juvenile alter ego, Pudge.

She also felt self-conscious about her traitorous thoughts of his body minutes before, as if he did know she'd been thinking of their first meeting. It added to her unease, and Alec's sudden change in mood threw her into total confusion.

Reluctantly she looked up to meet his gaze, unaware that her panic showed clearly on her expressive face. Her confusion only deepened when he hastily straightened. All animation left his face before he opened the door. Michelle allowed herself one more puzzled look at his face before she moved ahead of him into the room. His face was once more as remote as it had been all morning.

She shook her head to clear it, wondering if she'd imagined what had just happened. There was no time to dwell on it, though, because Alec was calling out a name over the hum of the computer.

"Yo," responded a cheerful tenor voice as a head with tousled brown hair popped out from behind the far side of the mainframe.

"Lew, the rep from Comtron is here. Have you got a minute?"

"Sure, no problem," replied the younger man with a smile on his pleasant face.

An answering grin spread across Michelle's lips as the lanky man ambled toward them. He was almost a double for her administrative assistant in Atlanta. Both Lew and her own Ernie looked like models for Norman Rockwell paintings. An open, honest face that always made her think of home, Mom, apple pie and Mickey Rooney movies. The only difference seemed to be the thickness of their glasses. While her assistant needed extremely thick lenses, Lew's black horn rims didn't look any stronger than her own reading glasses. She guessed he was several years younger than her, but she knew better than to equate age with intelligence.

"Hi, I'm Lew Rizzo," he announced as he stopped in front of them. His engaging grin and hearty handshake made up for the coolness of the other employees.

"Lew, this is Michelle Moens. You two will be working together on planning the upgrade and the new security program." Alec looked from his computer supervisor to Michelle with a frown.

"Moens? Oh, golly you're the head consultant," Lew exclaimed, swallowing quickly as his grin disappeared.

Michelle searched for a means to lessen his feelings of intimidation. She'd had a similar experience with Ernie until he discovered she'd skipped a few grades in

school, graduating high school and college two years
early, just as he had. It was an educated guess that Lew
had gone through the same excruciating experience of
being two years younger than all his classmates. "Hi,
Lew. Are you an egghead like me, or one of those de-
pressing average people who was never advanced in
school?"

His grin returned in a flash. "Gee, you, too? I was
nineteen when I graduated from college."

"You must be MENSA caliber. I was merely twenty,"
Michelle replied, trying to look crestfallen that she'd
only been smart enough to be moved ahead two years
instead of Lew's three.

"Well, yes, but I was twenty when I got out of grad-
uate school," he said, as though to reassure her that lack
of IQ points didn't matter to him.

"Excuse me, but you both lost me back at chief consultant," Alec interjected. Both Michelle and Lew
turned to him in surprise, their expressions showing
they'd forgotten he was there.

"Wow, Alec, we got the expert. She's the top consultant at Comtron," Lew informed him with excitement. "Don't you read the correspondence? M. H.
Moens is a big cheese."

"Really." Alec drew out the single word.

His whole body appeared to stiffen, Michelle
thought, as he regarded her through narrowed eyes. His
remote moodiness of the morning seemed almost am-
icable compared to his current mood. "That's very interesting," he commented. "We should be honored."

"Not really." Michelle hurriedly answered his frigid
statement in what she hoped was an offhand manner.
"We've been shorthanded recently due to two vacan-

cies and the overabundance of disaster damage in the Southwest, which has everyone out in the field. I'm the lucky one to have this job, since it means I don't have to climb over equipment torn apart by a tornado or slog through four feet of water."

"I see. We seem to have gotten the most for our money by mere chance," Alec noted, not sounding pleased about the circumstance. "Since that's the case, I'll leave you to talk binary codes. Lew can show you where to stash your gear."

"Hey, I'm sorry, Michelle," Lew sputtered as they both watched Alec turn abruptly and leave the room. "I don't know what his problem could be."

"Maybe his IQ is substandard and we offended him," she responded, her eyes still trained on the door Alec had managed not to slam as she'd expected. She bet herself that dinner tonight would be an extremely trying meal, then turned her attention to Lew and the Lindfors House computer. The former was a pleasant, uncomplicated change from his boss, and the latter usually only talked back when she wanted it to respond.

THE DIN of dozens of conversations filled the smoky living room Alec surveyed with a distant look. He spotted his host, Ted Landers, charming a vacuous brunette, and smiled humorlessly. Only Ted would turn a stockholders meeting into a cocktail party. If he wasn't one of his closest friends Alec would have stayed home tonight.

The thought of his apartment immediately brought forward the image of Michelle's sweet face from his subconscious. Not that it would have done him any good to be with her. He'd managed to make an ass of himself most of the day, at least the part of the day he'd spent with her. From his childish sulking on the way to the office to his adolescent retreat in the computer room, he'd been a certified jerk. There was also his crowning moment of idiocy, when he'd made that asinine comment about her name. Her confused, lost look still haunted him.

Taking a swallow of his drink, he considered finding a phone and reporting the computer problems directly to Jakob Hauser, chairman of Lindfors House Limited's board of directors. If he continued to irritate Michelle Moens, a discussion with Hauser would be inevitable. Alec was hoping to have the problems fixed and the anticomputer Hauser none the wiser. The man had been against the project from the start.

Alec was skating on thin ice, he knew, but after only forty-eight hours he was having difficulty keeping his mind on business and off the inviting form of Michelle Moens. An additional blow had been Lew's cheerful announcement that Michelle was an expert on the software Magda had tampered with to get her revenge. Would she be angry enough to report it to Hauser? The man would have a field day. Hauser would ask for Alec's resignation as president of the company that Axel Lindfors had built from a single storefront operation to a nationally known company. That was something Alec wasn't going to let happen.

Ted sauntered up with his attractive companion plastered to his side, and exchanged pleasantries with Alec about the business that had taken place earlier, while Alec ignored the come-hither smile of the woman. Abruptly he excused himself and left. He told

himself it was because the day had been long and tir-
ing. His early departure had nothing to do with the fact
Michelle had gone out to dinner with Lew Rizzo, can-
celling her plans to have dinner with *him*.

"LEW, ARE YOU out there?" Michelle called loudly from
her seat behind his desk. The green-and-white lines of
the printout before her were beginning to merge after
hours of constant reading since eight o'clock that
morning.

"Yo, just be a sec. Minnie and the girls are almost
done."

Michelle chuckled as she closed her eyes and sank
back in her chair to relax her lower-back muscles. As
she slowly rotated her neck to relieve the tension, she
decided Lew had been working with computers too
long. So had she, she admitted, since his answer made
perfect sense. When they'd begun the program checks
that morning Lew had despaired of his printer, saying
it sounded like hundreds of Minnie Mouse Rockettes
dancing their little rodent feet off. The bizarre word
picture helped distract her tired brain.

"Hey, I'm out there ruining my hearing and you're
taking a nap," Lew complained. He'd quickly overcome yesterday's intimidation. Michelle thought dinner together at Bennigan's had helped considerably.

She stopped rotating her neck and, with her head
cocked, only bothered to open her eyelids halfway. She
wondered why the rest of the Lindfors staff remained
distant, if not difficult. Dale Robeson, head of the billing department, came quickly to mind. The man had
scowled at her steadily when she'd asked about his de-

partment's procedures yesterday afternoon, and would only give unsatisfactory monosyllabic answers.

She looked at Lew's face in front of her, wondering if he would be any more helpful. He'd been somewhat vague about company procedures earlier. The printouts for the past month were missing and she needed them. She straightened in preparation to question him. Her sore back muscles caused her to wince.

"You okay?"

"I'm fine," she assured him, grimacing again from her stiffened shoulder muscles. "I got gung ho on my exercises this morning and sitting for three hours reading printouts hasn't helped my feeble muscles."

"I know just the thing," Lew exclaimed, an eager grin replacing his frown of concern. He bounded around the desk before Michelle could react.

"Hey," she managed when he pulled on her shoulders.

"Just relax. This will loosen you up."

She settled against the cushioned back of the chair as he began kneading the sore muscles at the base of her neck. As his thin hands worked their magic, she closed her eyes. When he hit one tender spot and worked away its stiffness, she murmured her approval. "Lew, that's wonderful."

Outside the office door Alec came to an abrupt halt at the sound of the softly murmured words. They were followed by Lew's chuckle and another satisfied feminine purr. A shaft of unfamiliar jealousy shot through him, quickly followed by anger. His ire was directed at the honey-haired woman who was disrupting his sleep and peace of mind. She'd sailed into the apartment only minutes after he'd returned last night and wished him a cheerful good-night. He'd had another sleepless night, while she'd been bright and sunny this morning at breakfast and on their walk to work.

He moved swiftly to the door of Lew's office, only to be brought up short by the sight of the couple behind the desk. Michelle was relaxed in the chair, her eyes closed, her oversize glasses halfway down her dainty nose. Her jade-green suit jacket was pushed aside, and Lew's bony fingers were kneading the smooth line of her shoulders. Alec clenched his hands, itching to put them around the younger man's throat, and none too gently. He could clearly remember the creamy smooth skin that lay beneath her pristine white blouse.

"Now, isn't that better?"

Lew's question broke the spell of Alec's morose trance. "I hate to interrupt your conference," he drawled, not bothering to control his caustic tone, "but I'd like to see when Ms Moens will be available this afternoon."

Michelle jumped to her feet, pulling her jacket up quickly and adjusting her glasses. For a moment she looked contrite, but when her brown eyes locked with Alec's narrowed gaze her whole body stiffened. She returned his glare, then spoke in a clipped tone.

"When will it be convenient for you, Mr. Lindfors?" she asked, emphasizing the formal term of address just as he had.

"Unless you have something important scheduled at three-thirty, we can meet in my office then," he answered with tight control. He wanted to pull her from behind the desk and shake her. Although it was irrational, he wanted to question her relationship with a youngster like Rizzo.

"Yes, three-thirty should be fine, Mr. Lindfors."

"Good, I'll have Britt pencil you in her book," he replied, and quickly turned on his heels. He had to get away from her before he did something embarrassing.

"Damn him."

"Michelle, cool down," Lew put in anxiously from where he sat on the credenza behind his desk. He hadn't moved since Michelle's precipitous rise from the chair had put him there. "He is the head honcho and I'm still on probation."

"Probation?" The single word brought her out of her frustrated glare at the empty doorway. She turned to Lew. "What do you mean 'probation'?"

"Just standard procedure for a new employee," he explained with a shrug and an easy smile. "I've only been here a month."

"You've only been here a month?"

"Yeah, Alec hired me when Magda Josefsen left," Lew answered, then cocked his head and frowned curiously. "Didn't you know that? I was teaching at De Vry until then."

"I see," she replied thoughtfully, leaning against the side of the desk. The woman's name rang a warning bell in her mind: she'd heard it somewhere but couldn't place it. More than likely one of the other employees had mentioned the former computer supervisor.

"Hey, what did you want to see me about, anyway?" Lew asked, jumping up, signaling he was ready to get back to work.

"The printouts from billing for the past month. Dale Robeson wasn't very helpful."

"If Dale doesn't have them, then Alec must," he replied, his voice dwindling in volume. "Uh, you can ask him during your meeting."

Michelle watched his sudden departure just as she had Alec's a few minutes previously. Lew hadn't met her eyes when he'd answered her. The niggling feeling of unease that had begun yesterday returned, even stronger than before.

Maybe she was becoming paranoid. There was probably a logical explanation for the missing printouts. She didn't have to know how recently Lew had been hired, either, for that matter. Alec may have assumed Lew would mention it, and the younger man thought the same.

"And yes, Michelle, there is a Santa Claus, too," she muttered as she sat down again. None of that accounted for the staff's hostility or Lew's sudden strange behavior. Her meeting with Alec should prove to be very interesting.

A few hours later she was almost looking forward to the meeting. Her eagerness stemmed from the list of questions on her clipboard, which she held securely against her chest as she walked briskly toward his office. She also welcomed the break from studying the various printouts and reports. Usually her background reading was done prior to an on-site visit, but her trips to other companies had disrupted her usual routine.

"Oh, Ms Moens," Britt Wahlberg greeted her with a smile as she entered the outer office. The gray-haired women had been with Lindfors House for years and maintained a rigidly structured office. "Mr. Lindfors has been held up with the new catalog layout. He said for you to make yourself comfortable in his office. If you'll come this way...."

Michelle smiled an acknowledgment and allowed the woman to usher her into Alec's office. She hadn't been in the room before this. With a curious eye she looked over her surroundings. The furnishings had the stark, clean lines of Lindfors House merchandise; beige walls and light gold carpet gave the area an open feeling; only the mass of papers on Alec's desk broke up the Spartan order of the room.

"I've brewed some fresh coffee. It's on the credenza," Britt offered, gesturing to the white china coffeepot and cups to her right. Her tone was much friendlier than the other employees in spite of her adherence to formalities. "Please have a seat. Mr. Lindfors shouldn't be long. Let me know if you need anything."

"Thank you, Britt. I don't think there'll be anything else," Michelle answered, returning the woman's smile before she left the room.

Michelle poured herself a cup of coffee and aimlessly wandered over to the single window behind Alec's desk. The view was limited to the building across the street and the street itself, some twenty stories below her. She turned her attention back to the room. A smile of amusement quirked her lips at the jumble of files and papers atop Alec's desk. Then her glance fell on a pair of pictures in a hinged frame that rose from the debris. Both subjects were familiar to her: Alec's parents and Jessica.

Michelle's smile widened as she took a closer look at her friend's photograph. She picked up the simple gold frame to confirm her suspicion that the picture had been taken at college at the end of their first year. It was actually one of a dozen that had been taken of the four suitemates, either alone or in groups next to the old oak tree. The picture Glynn had removed from behind Alec's bar at the apartment had no doubt been taken at the same time.

Her fond memories were interrupted as Alec came through the doorway. She put down the picture with a thud, feeling slightly guilty at being caught.

"She's very pretty," she began nervously as she walked around the end of his desk to stand next to the visitor's chair in which she should have been. His eyes never wavered from hers as he walked across the room to the spot she'd vacated.

"Yes, she is," he agreed, waiting for her to sit down before busying himself with the files on his desk. "That's my wife."

3

THIS IS IT, PREMATURE SENILITY, Alec decided while his pronouncement about Jess's picture echoed through the office. If not, Michelle was making him do the strangest things. There he stood, claiming his sister was his wife. The words had come out as an automatic defense.

The stupid game had become a habit ever since the first idiot gossip hound mistakenly reported Alec had gotten married four years ago. The erroneous story in the society column had been very amusing—and convenient—Alec recalled. Very convenient when his woman of the hour kept hinting she wanted a more permanent commitment from him and who disappeared quickly when he didn't deny the story. He never said he was married, and he'd never told an outright lie about his supposed marriage—until now.

He gave the cause of his current indiscretion a surreptitious look while pretending to be busy with the chaos on his desk. Other women had tried to wheedle and persuade him to disclose the merest hint about his marriage and the possibility of an imminent divorce. He'd always remained adamantly silent—neither admitting nor denying a word. And it was his private joke on the press, who continued to speculate on his nonexistent wife.

Those useless gossips who had no fit "news" to report constantly added to their own mistake. Alec—much to Glynn's disgust—savored every item about the "first" Mrs. Lindfors.

Today was the first time he'd given his newsprint wife a form or persona. He'd never even given the mythical woman a name. His little joke was much more amusing when simply a figment of the tattlemongers' imaginations.

Why now? He didn't bother to answer his rhetorical question as he ran out of paper to shuffle and sat down abruptly. He wasn't prepared to answer that question at the moment. He needed to concentrate on business. Michelle was there to question him about the computer, which was also treacherous ground. He had to center his full attention on that.

"Britt said you had some questions?"

How can he sound as if nothing is wrong? Michelle still couldn't believe what was happening. *And that's not my only question, buster!* She wanted to jump to her feet, point an accusing finger and shout, *That's your sister. I know her.* However, she was paralyzed by utter amazement, and could only grip the arms of her chair. Drawing on every ounce of professionalism in her body, she answered him. "Yes, there seem to be some printouts missing from billing for the past few weeks."

"Oh? Lew didn't have them?"

She wondered what he thought his cocky half smile would make her overlook. He appeared too innocently surprised, especially after his bold-faced fabrication. She certainly would not believe a word he said, not until she talked to Jessica. So he could flash that sexy dimple all he wanted.

"Both Dale and Lew thought you would have the printouts, since they couldn't locate them." She spoke each word precisely, while still attempting to make sense of his identification of Jessica. The missing print-out had bothered her all morning, but she found this new puzzle much more tantalizing than, though as confusing as, the computer problem.

Alec was saying something about checking his files, so Michelle nodded where it seemed appropriate. She couldn't remember what days Jessica went into San Francisco for her pottery class. If she couldn't reach Jessica before five o'clock Michelle wondered how to avoid Alec at the apartment until she was able to talk to her former roommate.

"Was there anything else we needed to discuss?"

Michelle stared at Alec for a minute, then collected her distracted thoughts. Ruthlessly she suppressed her first reaction: *How long have you been a pathological liar?* Instead she smiled stiffly and said, "No, I'll check back with you on the printouts."

Mechanically he returned her polite smile, hoping she wouldn't check back until Lew had had more time to find out what Magda had done to the computer software. If not, Alec would have to explain why there were no printouts. He stood and escorted Michelle to the door, shutting it firmly behind her.

Damn all women, he decided in disgust, and flung himself into his chair. He swiveled around to stare out the window. One woman had messed up his accounts program and the other was messing up his mind. He had to keep the problem quiet or the board of directors would have his hide. None of them wanted to automate in the first place, and continued to quibble about the mail-order expansion.

Well, he wasn't Axel Lindfors's son for nothing. He'd bullied the board into this and he'd find a solution. One solution came to mind, but he knew it wasn't in the realm of possibility. He knew he couldn't kidnap Michelle and lock her in his bedroom until Lew cleared up Magda's mess, no matter how appealing the idea was to him. As soon as he proofed the catalog layout, he was going to work out at the club.

He swung around and grabbed the phone. A few games of racquetball should do it, he determined with a grim smile. By the time Michelle Moens headed South again, he would be a physical and mental wreck.

EVERYONE IN THE OFFICE seemed to conspire to keep Michelle away from the phone. At first she'd thought of using the company's Watts line the moment she escaped from Alec's office. Unfortunately she couldn't shake Lew long enough even to dial the prefix code. Then she debated whether to call collect or charge it to her own number so the call wouldn't be recorded at Lindfors's office, which was all academic, because once she'd managed to lose Lew, she became involved in a lengthy discussion with Dale Robeson. Britt then brought her more files. By five o'clock Michelle was ready to scream for privacy.

She was beginning to identify strongly with Mata Hari as she made her escape from the office. She couldn't face Alec for the walk to the apartment. His startling disclosure wasn't the only reason. Her feet were beginning to ache from the punishing combination of high heels and concrete. Not just her feet hurt, either. In spite of Lew's helpful massage her whole body was slightly stiff from her abrupt renewal of her exercises that morning. By avoiding Alec she'd also have the luxury of a taxi ride to Marshall Fields.

Two hours later she returned triumphantly to the apartment with her purchases. She was now the proud owner of track shoes, complete with three stripes, designer logo and Velcro closures. Michelle hurried to the couch and pulled the shoe box from its sack. Tossing aside her other, less important packages, she sat down and slipped on her new shoes with a sigh of pleasure.

"New shoes, Miss Hal?" inquired Glynn. As usual, he'd suddenly appeared as if from nowhere.

She looked up guiltily, caught in the act of happily clicking her heels together. "Um-hmm, they should help out on my morning constitutional."

"Yes, ma'am, very smart," he agreed solemnly, but with a twinkle in his gray eyes. He gave the shoes an admiring look as she turned her ankle from side to side. "Might I make a suggestion?"

"Yes, of course," she responded, curious to know what a butler would advise about track shoes.

"They look new, Miss Hal."

She stared at him blankly for a moment, wondering why he was stating the obvious. Wrinkling her forehead, she tried to figure out what he was getting at. Then, smiling in comprehension, she exclaimed, "They look *brand*-new, Glynn."

"Exactly. Would you like me to season them for you?" he asked without batting an eye.

"Yes, please, Glynn," she agreed with equal aplomb, as if having a servant volunteer to dirty up her shoes was an everyday occurrence.

"Very good. Would you like something to eat after your shopping expedition?"

"No, thank you, Glynn. I grabbed a salad out since I didn't know how late I'd be." Michelle hoped she sounded pleasant. No longer diverted by her new purchases, she began calculating how to call Jessica undetected. Alec apparently wasn't home, so she tactfully had to find out where he was and how long he'd be gone.

"At least you had something nutritious. I'm not sure what Mr. Alec planned," Glynn volunteered with a note of displeasure. "He didn't say what time he'd be home when he called earlier and I hope he remembers to eat."

"Does he forget often?" Michelle asked the question before she'd had a chance to think. What, if not a woman, would make Alec forget about food? From Glynn's tone it sounded as though he didn't approve of his employer's current lady friend.

"Yes, Miss Hal, and staying out until all hours," the worried man answered, then hurried to qualify his words. "He spends far too many hours at the office— especially in the past month. All he has is coffee. I thought having a guest might keep him from working overtime."

"He's been very busy with the new mail-order business, I suppose," Michelle put in weakly. She felt somewhat guilty that Alec wasn't there. It was probably a coincidence, but she was sitting in the comfort of his home, hoping Alec wouldn't be in for hours. Of course, it was possible Glynn was blinded by his affection for his employer, and Alec was keeping late hours with one of his female companions.

"This mail-order venture is very important to him," Glynn agreed with a nod. "The board of directors has been very skeptical about the expansion because Alec's father never tried it."

"I see," Michelle murmured, although she really wasn't concentrating on Alec's problems with his board. Glynn knew more about Alec than almost anyone else and must therefore know about the mysterious Mrs. Lindfors. She had to work her way around subtly to the subject.

"Glynn, you know that picture frame that broke yesterday? How long will it take to get it fixed?" She kept her voice as casual as possible, trying, unsuccessfully, to read Glynn's expression.

"That's hard to say—framing is an art. Was there something you needed to know?"

"Actually, I saw a photograph of Mr. Lindfors's sister today in his office," Michelle explained cautiously, making sure she didn't admit to knowing Jessica. "I was curious if it was the same one."

"No, Miss Hal. The photograph behind the bar has two young ladies in it." Glynn's face didn't change. He could have been commenting on the weather. Michelle thought he'd seemed more animated discussing her track shoes.

She decided to forge ahead, even though talking to Glynn was a little like questioning a wooden Indian. "I thought it might be a picture of Alec's wife."

"No, Mr. Lindfors doesn't have any photographs of his wife," Glynn stated firmly. "Will there be anything else, Miss Moens?"

"No, Glynn, I think I'll just relax and read for a while, or maybe watch some television," she said in a meek voice, quashing the urge to apologize for being impertinent. She looked up at him inquiringly, almost checking to see if he approved of her activities, when she realized he was waiting for her track shoes. Flustered, she bent to take off her shoes, then handed them to him.

"Mr. Alec has a nice collection of video tapes if there's nothing of interest on the television," Glynn supplied, unbending slightly again. "I'll be in my room off the kitchen if you need anything."

If I need anything that's not a personal question about Mr. Alec Lindfors, Michelle added to herself as Glynn walked toward the kitchen, carrying her shoes with authority. She knew it was a gamble, so why was she so disappointed she hadn't learned more. Was there a Mrs. Alec Lindfors or not? she wondered, looking at the doorway through which Glynn had disappeared. The stoic Glynn hadn't contradicted her when she'd mentioned Jessica's photograph on Alec's desk and he'd said there were two young ladies in the missing photograph. He was also vague about when the frame would be fixed.

She had to be the second young lady. Impatiently she checked her watch and cursed the two-hour difference between California and Illinois. Her abortive attempt at pumping Glynn made her even more anxious to talk to Jessica, who never got home from her pottery class on Wednesdays until after six o'clock Pacific time, which meant she had an hour and a half to wait.

Restlessly she paced the living room. The picturesque cityscape didn't have its usually soothing effect, and as the minutes dragged by the first half hour, she rearranged every decoration in the room and flipped through each magazine. Finally she stopped in front of the entertainment center that housed the television, VCR and an extremely sophisticated stereo system.

She skimmed over the titles of Alec's videotape collection. When the names began to sink in through her distraction, Michelle began reading them over again. She was intrigued by the selection. He had all of Errol Flynn's swashbuckler epics, from *Captain Blood* to *Sea Hawk*. Next to them were Leslie Howard's *Scarlet Pimpernel*, and Ronald Coleman's *Prisoner of Zenda*, *Lost Horizon* and *Random Harvest*. The action films didn't surprise her, but the others were quiet, idealistic and highly romantic.

The Alec Lindfors she imagined should have a subscription to the Playboy channel and videotapes of the X-rated variety. The selection just didn't gibe with Glynn's workaholic employer. Still confused, she continued down the row of tapes. Every Fred Astaire and Ginger Rogers movie mixed with most of the screwball comedies of the late 1930s. Looking back over the titles, she realized there wasn't a movie made after the mid-forties.

After great deliberation she pulled out two tapes, her favorite Fred and Ginger and Mae West's wonderful *She Done Him Wrong*. Mae and Cary Grant would help her pass the time most enjoyably, and she wouldn't have to think any more about Alec, for now. She slipped the first tape in the VCR, then decided to change out of her shantung suit—old movies deserved comfortable clothes. She hastily exchanged her suit for her night-shirt and satin robe. Glynn was settled for the evening, and Alec was undoubtedly occupied the rest of the night with one of his lady friends, not working over-time.

Within minutes she was entranced by the naughty repartee of the buxom blond vamp. Poor Cary never stood a chance, but he enjoyed every minute of it. Without the interruption of commercials, the movie was over much too soon, but Michelle quickly in-serted *Top Hat* with Fred and Ginger and Edward Ev-erett Horton. She'd seen the movie countless times in college, when Patrice was working on a project about movie musicals. Nevertheless, as the master per-formed the title dance number, her absorption was so complete that she jumped when the phone rang on the glass end table next to her.

Without taking her eyes from the screen, she lifted the receiver on the third ring.

"Finally! I've been trying to track you down since Monday. Happy birthday, you rat," sang out a femi-nine voice before Michelle had a chance to utter a sound.

"Lindfors residence," she answered, for lack of any-thing else to say, wondering if this was a wrong num-ber or one of Alec's groupies.

"Good heavens, ole Glynn's been traded in for a new model," the woman answered with a chuckle. "Is Alec there?"

A grin broke across Michelle's face as she gave her full attention to the caller. The voice was more than famil-

iar. "Is this Mrs. Philip Benedict, alias Mrs. Alec Lindfors?"

There was a gasp at the other end of the phone, then
a husky chuckle. "Hal, is that you? Did I dial the wrong
number again? What are you talking about?"

Michelle laughed in delight at the usual string of
rapid-fire questions. "What does 'love and lots of hugs,
Jess,' remind you of, Fred?"

"I always sign my letters that way. Wait a minute, I
didn't call Atlanta. I remember dialing 312. What are
you doing in the company's apartment?"

"Lindfors House has Comtron equipment, and your
big brother has a problem that only a real pro could
handle," she replied, still laughing at her friend's confusion. "After all these years I finally meet the brother
of legend and song, only to discover that you're a biga-
mist. One of my closest friends, and you never told me."

"What?"

"Alec showed me a very charming, vintage picture
of you this afternoon—you were wearing my cameo
necklace, I might add—and told me it was his wife."

"But he's not marr— Oh, gawd, I forgot."

"Forgot what?" Michelle felt light-headed as she
waited for her friend's next words.

"It was all a mistake. I didn't realize he was still doing
it."

"Doing what, for pete's sake?" she practically
shouted in her impatience over Jessica's hesitation.

"Well, it started when Alec and I went out to dinner
not too long after Philip and I got engaged. I was bug-
ging him about whether he was ever going to get married. He made some silly toast to his wife, whoever she

might be. When I got back home he sent a clipping from a gossip column in one of the papers."

"Don't stop now," Michelle prompted when Jessica paused suddenly.

"I have to breathe," the other woman protested. "Apparently one of those tacky gossipmongers overheard us and assumed I was Alec's wife. There was a brief paragraph speculating about his mystery marriage. I didn't realize he went along with it."

"Went along with it? That lech is notorious for a string of affairs while keeping his mysterious, estranged wife safely in reserve." Michelle couldn't keep the caustic edge from her voice as she remembered the bitter words she'd snapped at Alec in her anger.

"I'm a forsaken woman and I didn't even know it." Jessica laughed, then stopped abruptly when her friend's tone registered. "Hal, he hasn't, um, I mean—"

"Oh, yes, he's tried, my innocent friend," Michelle assured her with a sharp laugh, "but he's in for a big surprise."

"Well, whatever it is, he deserves it. I wonder if Mother knows about this. After all, she does live in town when she isn't traveling. You know, if his hair wasn't so light I'd give him a lecture that would turn it completely white."

"Oh, Fred, I do love you," Michelle exclaimed as a noise at the door caught her attention. "Listen, I'll have to get back to you on that. I don't have enough data."

"Alec's home," Jessica sang out perceptively at her friend's brisk tone of voice. "You call me back at noon your time tomorrow or else. I need to find out just what's going on there. Now give me a loving send-off, sweetie."

Michelle's smile extended from ear to ear as she remembered some of their college ploys that had confused their dates. "I miss you, too, sweetie. By, now."

The thud of the receiver in its cradle was the only sound in the room. Michelle watched Alec's reflection in the window out the corner of her eye while she fiddled with the remote control. He hadn't moved since he'd entered the room. His tie was loosened and his hands were shoved into his trousers, so that the material stretched tautly over his thighs as he stood with his legs apart.

With a calculated move Michelle looked around and feigned surprise at his presence, then turned off the VCR. "Oh, good evening."

She was slightly uneasy when, instead of responding, he continued to stare at her when she stood. Her only option seemed to be a strategic retreat to her room. Preoccupied with her secrets, she was unaware of the appeal of her lush figure, snuggly wrapped in golden satin, as she crossed the room.

"Who's 'Fred'?"

His abrupt question stopped Michelle in mid-step. She turned halfway to face him. Her inquiring look masked her agitation as she watched him move toward her with a menacing gait. Alec couldn't possibly remember his sister's nickname, she reasoned, as the four friends rarely used them with outsiders.

"An old friend," she replied, her eyes glued to the loosened knot of his tie. Swallowing to clear the lump in her throat, she groped for something to change the subject. Her words seemed trapped in her throat when he curved his hand around her jaw. Lightly Alec rubbed his thumb again her bottom lip.

"May I be an old friend?" he murmured, bringing her startled brown eyes up to meet his intense gaze. The rough texture of his voice sent tiny sparks shooting down Michelle's spine. Her mouth felt as dry as a desert, and another convulsive swallow didn't help. Mesmerized by his eyes, she wet her lips. But when her tongue encountered the pad of Alec's thumb, she quivered from the almost electric shock.

He continued to demolish her free will by raising his left hand to her hair, deftly removing the hair pins that secured her pompadour. His long fingers were threaded now into the reddish gold tresses, and she desperately tried to think of a diversion. His gaze was centered on her lips, his head bending slowly.

"You've been drinking," she accused in a hesitant voice, as she caught a whiff of alcohol on his breath. The effect of her defensive accusation was diminished when her voice tapered off into a squeak.

"Only enough to try to forget the feel of your delicious body next to mine."

Her gasp of surprise was cut off by the gentle nibbling of his lips. The touch was fleeting as he began to place feathery kisses over her bemused face. "Do you know, not very many men have an opportunity to have a fantasy come to life? Waking up with you in my arms was definitely a living dream."

Heat seemed to suffuse Michelle's bloodstream as his beautifully chiseled lips coaxed hers apart. She closed her eyes to savor the myriad sensations assaulting her as he explored the moist sweetness of her mouth. Willingly she allowed him to pull her aroused body more firmly against his. With a soft moan, she acknowledged her pleasure in the proof of his desire when he held her against the cradle of his thighs.

Knowledgeable hands trailed down her back over the thin satin of her robe, seeming to burn away the fabric. Her traitorous mind recalled the same feeling against her skin that first morning in Alec's bed. The dangerous, provocative memory only heightened her need for the man holding her. Instinctively she trailed her fingers over his chest, seeking the buttons of his shirt. She delighted in his slight tremor of response.

"Oh, Michelle, what are you doing to me?" Alec groaned as he freed her mouth to explore the pulse beating wildly at the base of her throat. His voice stilled her hands. "Don't stop, sweetheart. I want you to touch me and want me as much as I want you."

Boldly Michelle tugged at the knot of his tie before returning to the stubborn buttons of his shirt. She had trouble concentrating while Alec nuzzled her throat, so to distract him, she playfully nibbled at his ear.

Alec was as impatient as she was. Abruptly he removed his jacket and disposed of his shirt. His tie joined his jacket on the floor, along with two buttons from his shirt. Michelle expressed her gratitude by seeking his addictive lips just as the jarring ring of the phone filled the room.

"Alec, the phone," she whispered against his mouth.

"Glynn will answer it."

"It might be important," Michelle insisted, trying to regain some control over her spinning senses.

"Glynn is trained to know what's important and what isn't." He laughed softly before stopping any further conversation with a burning kiss.

"Mr. Lindfors, you're wanted on the telephone," Glynn interrupted in a grating voice just as Alec tightened his arms around Michelle again.

All acquiescence left Michelle at the sound of the other man's voice. She stepped back quickly, her reflexes a second faster than Alec's. For a moment she was held by the clouded passion in his ultramarine eyes. Glynn cleared his throat and broke the spell. She retreated to the sanctuary of her room as an unhappy Alec turned toward the phone, muttering under his breath.

She shut the door securely behind her, leaning against it to ensure her security. Over the sound of her agitated breathing, Michelle could hear muffled footsteps in the other room. She sagged against the cool wood, hearing Alec's muted voice as he answered the phone.

Slowly she eased away from the door, her steps quickening as she neared the bathroom. There was little relief from the cool washcloth across her face. After a steadying breath, she met her own troubled gaze in the mirror. Dark, stormy brown eyes dominated her flushed face, framed by loosened tendrils of hair. Tentatively she touched her swollen lips, but abruptly dropped her hand to her side to dismiss the sight of her trembling fingers.

"Fool," she accused her reflection, pulling the pins from her disheveled hair and dragging a brush through it. The usually soothing action did not silence her self-condemnation. Minutes later she settled in bed, only to stare restlessly at the ceiling.

Against the grainy pattern of the plaster overhead she pictured the tortures that should be inflicted on lying men who didn't comprehend the meaning of fidelity. Two men were the leading candidates. Alec was standing only a few steps behind Stuart Packard.

With agitated movements she remembered handsome, charming and lying Stuart. He'd entered her life at a low point. Two of her closest friends had moved to other cities; one was transferred and the other married. Stuart filled a gap of loneliness. She'd foolishly ignored hints that he wasn't what he seemed. The relationship had gone on for seven months before she'd learned the truth from Stuart's wife, who arrived on her doorstep.

The realization that she'd been a married man's mistress had devastated Michelle. For months she didn't socialize, burying herself in her work to forget her stupidity and to avoid her acquaintances' knowing looks. Almost a year later she was offered her current job, and with some of her self-confidence restored, she cautiously resumed a social life.

Michelle was determined she would never again play the role of the other woman. She had to clarify her conversation with Jessica before deciding what to do about Alec. If he wasn't married, he should be hung by his thumbs for the anguish he'd undoubtedly caused the women he'd callously lied to. She'd have liked to give him a piece of her mind, but he'd probably laugh in her face. He was, after all, only amusing himself with her because she was close at hand.

During their brief acquaintance Alec had already given her cause for chronic insomnia. She couldn't reconcile her emotional and physical reactions to a man whose life-style she despised. After three years of avoiding any emotional involvement, she was attracted to a man who was either married or a liar, but definitely a philanderer.

Rolling over on her stomach, she gave an envious sigh. If only she were tall and built like Patrice or Jessica, maybe she could teach the devious Mr. Lindfors a lesson. A five-feet-four-inch chubbette was never cast as the femme fatale in the old movies.

ALEC WALKED QUICKLY across the darkened kitchen, feeling sorry for his brother-in-law. He always thought his sister was slightly crazy, and her phone call only reinforced it. She'd giggled continuously throughout the entire conversation once she'd wished him happy birthday. However, his mind hadn't been on Jessica's prattle. His mind and body had still been reacting to the taste and feel of Michelle in his arms again.

He felt every one of his thirty-eight years, he decided as he stopped at the closed door on the far side of the kitchen. A bar of light showing from beneath the door signaled that Glynn was still awake. Alec rapped with two knuckles, trying to think of what he was going to say. When the door swung open and he met Glynn's inquiring expression, he was still at a loss.

"Was there something you needed, sir?"

"Do you still keep that bottle of Scotch in your nightstand, Glynn?" Alec asked as he tried to soften his old friend's mood. The other man was standing as stiff as a poker and looked very unapproachable.

"Yes, sir," Glynn replied, and stepped aside to allow the younger man to enter his room.

Alec made himself comfortable in his usual armchair while Glynn retrieved the liquor stash and two glasses. Glynn returned and handed his employer a glass with a mere finger of liquid, then sat down, too. Alec raised his eyebrows questioningly.

"You've had a head start, sir."

"Knock off the servile nonsense, Homer," Alec answered, using Glynn's first name with a mocking smile. "You always become more subservient when you want to annoy me. I went to work out at the club and only had two drinks on Rush Street on the way home, so I'm not quite ready to pass out."

"Yes, Alec," Glynn returned with a slightly skeptical twist to his mouth. It was apparent he was refraining from commenting on his employer's choice of recreation. He took a drink from his glass, keeping an eye on Alec's, which remained still.

"How long have we known each other, Homer?"

"About fourteen years."

"Mmm-hmm." Alec nodded as he watched the placid face across from him. Glynn certainly remembered his lines perfectly after years of the same dialogue, which had begun the night of Axel Lindfors's funeral. "How many times have I fired you since I pulled your drunken carcass out of that gutter in Tokyo?"

"Before or after we left the service?"

"Altogether will be fine."

"Twenty-nine."

"Did I miss one?"

"The last time was when I told Ms Josefsen you were at a reception at the Drake, just two months ago."

"Ah, yes," Alec replied with a nod, and took a sip of his drink. He grimaced because he hated Scotch, but this had become a ritual in the past ten years. "This should mark a new record, then."

"You're right. You've never fired me more than twice in six months before," Glynn agreed, without looking the least bit disturbed.

"I realize tonight may have been an error in judgment on your part, seeing as I've never had a woman here alone," Alec continued smoothly, his eyes trained on Glynn's solemn face, "but what was she doing in my bed in the first place? You notice I did overlook that at first."

"It was Sunday, sir. You usually stay at home all weekend, so I naturally didn't expect you." Not a flicker of emotion, guilt or innocence, crossed the older man's face.

Alec narrowed his eyes in concentration. Only the slip into formality gave away anything that could be called suspicious. Unfortunately Glynn used formalities to show indignation at times.

"Alec, there are two points I'd like to clarify. The first is that I've been fired again, so the count is now thirty?" He paused briefly and waited while the other man nodded slowly. "The other is perhaps merely semantics, but Miss Michelle is the first lady who's been here alone."

Alec didn't answer immediately as the words sank in. He lowered his eyes from Glynn's penetrating gray stare to study his drink. The statement wasn't really one of semantics, but one of truth. The disquieting thought wouldn't help him sleep any better tonight, especially when it was apparent the lady had a champion in residence.

"I hope you aren't planning on asking about my intentions just yet, because I honestly don't know them." He came back on the defensive because it was awkward being chastised by an employee, no matter how good a friend. Also, he wasn't drawing solace from talking to his old friend as usual.

"Not yet. You'll tell me when you figure it out, I'm sure," Glynn gave him a tolerant smile that grated on his already-raw nerves.

Alec sprang to his feet and thrust his glass at the other man. "I don't think this has really eased my mind the way it was supposed to."

His muttered comment was ignored as Glynn placed the glasses on his nightstand. "Is oatmeal all right for breakfast tomorrow?"

"Yes, that's fine," he agreed with an absent wave of his hand, not really giving a damn about food.

"Oh, sir," Glynn called a second later as Alec opened the door, "I'll be washing some of Miss Michelle's lingerie in the morning—"

"Did you think I might want to help?" He snapped out the question, turning back to face the older man.

"Certainly not. I just wanted to make sure your handkerchiefs were all in the hamper," came the icy reply, matching an extremely rigid posture. "I do the Irish linen ones by hand."

"Terrific, Glynn. Just terrific. That should help me sleep much easier." Alec turned to leave once more, visions of Michelle's lingerie in his handkerchief drawer. Quickly they escalated to thoughts of Michelle without her lingerie. "And I get to look forward to gruel for breakfast, too."

Without a backward glance he stomped across the kitchen. There was nowhere he could escape Michelle. His peace of mind would have deteriorated even more if he'd seen Glynn leaning against the doorjamb, shaking with silent laughter.

ONLY THE LUNCHTIME skeleton crew remained when Michelle stealthily returned from the rest room. She'd hidden there for ten minutes to make sure Lew had gone to lunch. He was a nice man, but she didn't want him around to overhear her phone call to Jessica.

The morning had passed with agonizing slowness, and she was practically a nervous wreck. Neither Alec nor Glynn had spoken more than two words at breakfast. Even her satisfaction with her new track shoes, which had allowed her to keep pace with Alec, was overshadowed by her calculations on how to call Jessica in private.

She found the computer room empty, and sighed in relief. Michelle hurried into Lew's office, shutting the door for extra security. Impatiently she waited for the operator to complete her credit-card call. When a male voice answered the ring, she almost groaned out loud. Philip *would* pick today to leave late for work.

"May I speak to Jessica? This is Michelle."

"Michelle, how are you?"

Philip's enthusiastic greeting grated on her nerves.

"How are things in the sunny South?"

"Fine, the last time I saw it—I'm on the road right now." She wondered how to get him off the phone. Sometimes he'd stay on for ten or fifteen minutes before relinquishing the receiver. Then in the background she heard a feminine voice.

"Hey, Jess, don't tickle. It's not fair. I don't get to talk to gorgeous strawberry blondes everyday," Philip complained before addressing Michelle again. "I think she's anxious to talk to you, but I demand equal time next call."

"Yes, yes, fine, Philip," she answered automatically, then relaxed when Jessica took the receiver. "You could have warned me."

"I would have if I'd known he'd be here. He came home for some special concoction for somebody's sick bonsai."

"Is the coast clear?" Michelle asked, dismissing Philip's landscape business and anxious to learn more about Alec's marital status. "Did I understand you last night? Alec is not married?"

"As of ten-fifteen central time last night he wasn't," Jessica answered promptly. "Just what he was doing before I called back would be interesting to know, however."

"Pardon?" Michelle closed her eyes and braced herself for what was sure to come—the third degree. It was Jessica's phone call that had interrupted them last night.

"He must have been doing something strenuous," Jessica continued, then paused for a response that didn't come. "Why is that, you ask? Because he was breathing rather heavily. If Glynn hadn't answered first, I would have thought I'd connected with an obscene breather."

"He must have run to take the call," Michelle improvised, then decided to compound her lie for good measure. "I went to bed right after I spoke to you."

"Alone?"

"Of course alone. Your brother's not that desperate." She slumped in her chair and held the phone away from her ear. She could still hear Jessica's rather creative swearing very clearly, although she wasn't sure at whom it was directed.

"Michelle Henrietta Moens, you're going to drive me stark raving mad one of these days," Jessica finally said once she'd finished venting her emotions. "You're not going to start that nonsense again. Damn that jerk Stuart for ruining our four years of reconditioning."

Michelle dreaded what was coming. Jessica would begin the recitation to build up her ego, as she had countless times in college. "Now, Fred—"

"Don't try to soften me up."

"But—"

"How tall are you?"

"I'm five-feet-four-inches tall," she said with a re-signed sigh. Jessica was going to make her go through the entire pep talk. Her friends had devised it when she'd refused to go to a freshman dance. Self-conscious about her age and still not adjusted to losing her baby-fat figure, she'd been able to get out of weekend visits to the campus bars. However, Jessica had finally realized that Michelle's evasions were a cover for her lack of confidence in meeting men.

"Are you overweight?"

"Five pounds from being on the road so much."

"Which means you'll lose ten pounds when you get home. Are you usually overweight for your height and frame?"

"No. Now come on, Jess—"

"Have you ever worn a size larger than a twelve since high school?"

"No, but—"

"Is my brother an incredibly sexy man?"

"Yes, but—" Michelle cut short her words when the other woman laughed triumphantly. "You rat. That was really low."

"I never fight fair, especially when I know you wouldn't have told me otherwise," Jessica responded without remorse. "Besides, that's much more interesting than getting depressed reciting your measurements, which was next on the agenda."

"Depressed?"

"Hal, sweetie, have you ever considered the irony of the situation? Your dresses are better built on the hanger than I am," the other woman answered good-naturedly.

"Oh." Michelle couldn't think of anything else to say. Jessica had never complained before this.

"Exactly. Now you think my big brother is incredibly sexy, and he's not married. So what are you going to do about it?"

"Me?" Michelle squeaked, still trying to recover from Jessica's admission of envy.

"Of course *you*. It's absolutely perfect," her friend announced gleefully. "You're staying at the corporate apartment with him. Proximity is a wonderful catalyst for seduction."

"Seduction? Jess, have you been smoking some of Philip's shrubs?"

"No, silly. All you have to do is give Alec that sweet come-hither smile of yours and let him wine and dine you a little. When he goes in for the kill, you laugh in his face."

"You're saying you want me to lead your brother on, then stomp all over him?" She couldn't believe Jessica actually wanted her to callously set out to hurt Alec, or that Jessica thought her brother would be tempted by her.

"Don't go soft on me. This will only give Alec's conceit a well-deserved kick," his sister assured her ruthlessly.

"Jes-si-ca-a," Michelle whined, giving her name an added syllable.

"Okay, here we go again," Jessica grumbled at her friend's cowardly response. "Has my brother been lying abut being married or at least let the lie continue?"

"Yes," Michelle answered tentatively, wondering if anyone ever won an argument with Jessica.

"Is that fair to the women he's dated under false pretenses?"

"No."

"Shouldn't he have the same stress as any other single male?"

"Well, yes, I suppose." Michelle's reply was hesitant as she realized Jessica was beginning to make sense. At least she was making sense about why Alec deserved to be tricked. Aware that she was losing the argument about seducing Alec, Michelle said, "You didn't even know he was still pretending to be married until yesterday."

"Don't change the subject, Hal. Now—"

"Look, you have to know a dozen women in Chicago who could get back at him."

"None of them are living with him and are as trustworthy as my best friend," Jessica answered in a gloating tone as she played her trump card. "Check in every few days and call collect, or at least phone during lower rates. This call's going to cost you a fortune. Bye, now."

Michelle stared at the receiver in disbelief. The war was over and she hadn't even loaded her gun. Somehow she was supposed to take Jessica's sexy-as-hell, Scandinavian-stud brother and teach him a lesson. Jessica made it sound so simple. *When he goes in for the kill, you laugh in his face.*

I have a snowball's chance at doing that, she decided as she listlessly replaced the receiver. Then she did the only thing that made sense. She crossed her arms on the desk, put down her head and groaned. She knew it really wasn't constructive, but it kept her from screaming at the top of her lungs.

After a few minutes, Michelle knew she had to start behaving like a grown woman. She straightened and gave herself a shake, deciding that Jessica was a very unnatural sister and friend.

She chuckled as she pulled out her purse and track shoes to prepare for lunch. Life around Jessica was never dull, she mused, and chuckled again as she neared the end of the hallway. She heard voices in the reception area around the corner, but was preoccupied with her thoughts until she heard her name mentioned.

"She'd better be less trouble than his last lady friend, whom he tried to pass off as a computer expert."

Michelle immediately recognized the disgruntled voice of Dale Robeson. After three no-win encounters with the surly head of accounts, she had no trouble placing him.

"Now, Dale, we don't know if she's anything more than the Comtron rep," Katrin answered, but her words didn't hold much conviction.

"Katrin, get your head out of the sand. You were the last one to figure out Mr. Boss-man was playing patty cake with Her Highness Magda Josefsen."

"That's because Princess Magda didn't waste her time with lowly receptionists." Katrin's voice was dripping with sweetness. "She only deigned to speak to big, strong male department heads and company presidents."

"Katrin, I had lunch with the woman *once*," Dale said, a defensive edge to his tone. "That was over three months ago, for pete's sake. Can we drop it?"

"Just count yourself lucky Alec fired her before you worked your way up to dinner. He wasn't the only one who was tired of her," Katrin returned quickly. "However, Michelle Moens is totally different from the high-and-mighty Miss Josefsen. She's nice and—"

"Don't get too worked up until you know where your Ms Moens is staying during her visit." Dale broke in with a triumphant laugh. "Your nice, friendly Ms Moens is staying at the company apartment and she's not staying there alone. The boss has been in town all week and the office lottery is taking bets on whether he goes home to Lake Forest on the weekend."

"Oh, Dale," groaned the receptionist, "just because Magda was his mistress doesn't mean Michelle is sleeping with him."

"Let's just forget the whole thing and go to lunch," Dale said, and gave a heavy sigh. "Switch the calls through to Britt's office, okay?"

4

MICHELLE REMAINED as still as a statue as she listened to the sound of Dale's and Katrin's retreating footsteps. She wasn't sure she could move even if she'd wanted to, after what she'd just heard.

Dale Robeson wasn't her favorite person in Chicago, but now she knew part of the reason for his irritability. He had her marked as one of Alec's playmates. Still, that didn't give him the right to interfere with her work by withholding his department's printouts. She started walking toward the entrance, then stopped in the middle of the now-empty reception area. She wasn't really hungry anymore. However, she had to get out of the office, so she decided to take a walk by the river.

As the elevator made its descent a fantasy of throwing Alec Lindfors's body into the Chicago River formed in her mind. She idly wondered how much it would take to weigh down his muscular six-foot frame inside a burlap bag. When she emerged from the office building, the sunshine of the spring day didn't lighten her mood. She was still envisioning cement overshoes as she traversed the few blocks and trotted down the concrete steps to the water's edge.

She walked on, lost in thought until she came to a bench, where she sat down and stared across the brown waters. Jessica's dare, she mused, was beginning to appeal to her. Alec deserved to be made a fool of, if only to punish him for his treatment of the unfortunate woman he'd ruthlessly fired. Not to mention that his lies about being married were no better than Stuart's claim of being single. Although Alec didn't have a wife hidden in the background, both he and Stuart were selfish men who thought only of their own needs.

Her dark thoughts of Stuart brought back part of her recent conversation with Jessica. *Damn that jerk Stuart for ruining our four years of reconditioning.* The implication finally sank in.

Her friends had indeed reconditioned her. Fifteen years ago, she'd been a shy, overly self-conscious teenager, but due to their loving and demanding efforts, she'd been able to pursue her computer interests in the male-dominated classrooms. Armed with newfound self-confidence and a hard-won MBA, she hadn't batted an eye during the stressful interviews with corporate head hunters upon graduation.

For three years she'd worked at a job she loved and enjoyed an active social life. Then Stuart Packard had come into her life. He'd been her first adult love, and she'd committed herself to him in her only physical relationship. The discovery that he was married had made her feel used, betrayed.

Until this moment she hadn't realized how much she'd let herself regress due to *his* selfishness. She'd retreated within herself, taking Stuart's perfidy as her fault. The stigma of being a married man's mistress, no matter how innocent she was, overruled other rational thoughts. The way she saw it, she'd only been attractive enough for a married man, not good enough to be anything but the "other woman."

"Damn him. Damn both of them," she muttered fiercely, including Alec in her condemnation. He was another uncaring Lothario. His amorous exploits were affecting her work. Dale Robeson and the others at Lindfors House had passed judgment on her without any consideration for her qualifications. She was automatically linked with poor Magda, whom he'd cast aside like an old shoe when he'd grown tired of their affair. Her anger quickly rekindled as she considered the influence of this second libidinous male on her life. Another man's lies were making her a victim again. Only this time, he would take the rightful blame.

The sound of voices close by caused Michelle to look up. A tourist excursion boat was invading the silent river channel to her right, and the chattering voices from beneath the blue-and-white striped canvas top carried easily over the water. Brought out of her dark reverie, she checked her lapel watch. A half hour had passed since her angry departure from the office. She stood up and straightened her Chanel-style jacket, as if gearing for battle. With squared shoulders, she determinedly retraced her steps to Lindfors House Limited. Alec Lindfors had a lot to answer for, and she would see to it he learned his lesson. Even Jessica might be surprised by the results.

The walk back and the elevator ride took only minutes. She barely acknowledged Katrin's greeting on her way through the reception area. There was a single objective in her mind: the computer room. Only two, unguardedly friendly people were employed by Mr. Alec Lindfors: the precise Britt and good old Lew.

She barely waited for the computer-room door to shut behind her. "Lew, I want to see you in your office. Now!"

She stalked into the cubicle and waited with her hands on her hips. Lew's head popped up from behind the terminal at the far side of the computer. He trotted across the room, but stopped dead in the doorway when he saw her rigid stand, her left foot tapping a staccato beat.

"Something wrong, Michelle?" he asked with a wary look.

"Sit," she replied, pointing to the desk chair. No other words were needed to enforce her terse command and gesture.

He shuffled around the far side of his desk, eyeing her confusedly, then slowly lowered himself into the chair. Slumping, he looked sheepishly at Michelle as she moved to stand directly in front of him. She widened her stance, placing both hands back on her hips.

"Why did Magda Josefsen leave this company?"

Her softly spoken words caused Lew to lean forward in the chair. He swallowed convulsively, but didn't answer. His brown, wing-tip clad feet shifted uneasily. He dropped his gaze to study his corduroy-covered knees, which were bent at perfect right angles.

"Well?"

Lew jerked his head up at her impatient prompting. He shifted his weight, leaning heavily to his left side. "She was fired."

Michelle pinned him with a speaking look, wordlessly letting him know his hesitant sentence was inadequate.

"I don't know all the gory details," he said in a rush, clearly distressed that she was so determined.

"So tell me what you do know." She relaxed slightly, easing up in the hope that Lew would be less reticent. She perched on the corner of the desk with a feigned air of nonchalance.

"This is all secondhand," he began cautiously as he sat back in his chair. "She was spending more time keeping track of Alec than she was on her job. The last few weeks she was here they had some dandy arguments."

"And?" Michelle prodded when he stopped to swallow. She ignored the pleading look in his soft, spaniel eyes.

"He fired her so she'd leave him alone," he finally managed with a guilty look, unaware he was simply confirming what she already knew. "She left, but she also let everyone know why."

"I see," she answered softly, trying to pretend his words hadn't extinguished a tiny flicker of hope. She hopped to her feet in what she hoped was a cheerful manner and spoke brightly to counteract her depressed state. "Well, now that that's settled, let's get back to work. I still need the accounts printouts."

When Lew didn't answer, she focused her attention back on his dejected figure. The ominous quiet continued as she watched him fidget still more in the chair. "Lew?"

He looked up reluctantly, a flush spreading from the collar of his tattersall plaid shirt. More than ever he looked like a puppy who knew he was going to be punished for the ultimate sin and have his nose rubbed in it. "The printouts are no good. She did something to the program, so all the accounts are delinquent. Dale and his staff have been doing manual billing, which has also screwed up shipping."

He broke off when Michelle made a strange noise in her throat. She wasn't aware of the sound until his eyes widened in surprise. Unclenching her balled fists, she groaned inwardly at the thought that she'd actually felt sorry for the vindictive Magda only a half hour before. In her vengeance, the woman had damaged Michelle's brainchild. No one was going to destroy her creation, and certainly not one of Alec Lindfors's cast-off women.

Slowly she relaxed her body. First she had to think rationally about how to solve the immediate problem of salvaging her program. Later she'd consider how to tell Alec exactly what she thought of his part in this mess.

"Tell me what you've done so far," she ordered briskly, not letting Lew's hangdog expression undermine her resolve. After he gave her a brief rundown, she nodded and took off her jacket to prepare for the onerous task. "All right, bring me all the hard copy of what you've done. We'll retrace your steps first, then we'll see what we can do. Between the two of us, I doubt one of Alec's has-beens stands a chance of outsmarting us."

She watched Lew shuffle out the door and wondered if he believed her. Her self-doubts began to resurface, but she ruthlessly suppressed them. This was her turf, and she knew she was one of the top people in her field. The fact that three other companies had tried to hire her away from Comtron was proof of that. Whatever sympathy she felt for Magda was gone, leaving only anger that the woman's revenge was harming more than her intended victim. Once Michelle fixed the problem, she'd confront Alec and make sure his personal life would never backlash on her business again.

ALEC SLAMMED DOWN the phone receiver and swiveled his padded leather chair around to face the window. He stared straight ahead without really seeing the brick-and-glass facade of the building across the street. His mind replayed the conversation he'd abruptly ended.

The Louisiana distributor had just cut back on his order and threatened to discontinue both the glassware and pewter orders. Alec wasn't surprised. This was the fifth such call he'd received since the computer had gone haywire. It was a miracle only five of his thirty regions had called. However, he knew it was only a matter of time before the others would complain. Dale had told him this morning that his department was now three weeks behind in their attempts to keep up without the computer.

With the board meeting only a week away, he cursed the day Jan Josefsen had recommended his niece for the position of computer department head at Lindfors House. As Jan was an old friend of his father's, Alec had done the courteous thing and interviewed his niece, Magda. The woman had actually been more than qualified for the job. He ignored the old adage of never hiring friends, relatives or a combination of the two. Unfortunately he discovered that beneath her beautiful shell, Magda Josefsen was as cold and calculating as the machinery she controlled.

His image of the tall, willowy blonde was quickly replaced by the memory of the softer curves of Michelle. There was nothing cool about that lady, from the warm honey red of her hair to the fire generated by her kiss. She could warm a man by her mere presence, something Magda could never do by any stretch of the imagination in her determined, analytical search for a husband. He was sure Michelle would never become the nuisance the blonde had been.

The petite computer expert had filled his thoughts too often for his peace of mind since her arrival. He'd been honest with Glynn the previous night; he didn't know what his intentions were. All he knew was that he wanted Michelle in his bed again. This time it wouldn't be an innocent night of sleep, but a night of passion that would imprint his body on hers. Her blood would sing at his touch, just as his did whenever she entered the room.

However, he'd have to be patient. He swung his chair back to the desk to check his calendar. Tomorrow was the Wilkins' wedding anniversary at the Palmer House. That was just the atmosphere he needed to continue his campaign. Then he swore under his breath at the need for all this plotting. He was a veteran of seduction who should know how to handle any situation with a desirable woman. For a brief moment he considered the fact that in spite of his lack of interest Magda had been eager to pursue him.

Too eager, he recalled grimly. As eager as he was to begin a physical relationship with Michelle. After all, what other kind of relationship was there? That was why he'd left the matter of his erroneous marriage go uncorrected all these years; it left him free to enjoy himself without any complications. So why did he have this urge to tell Michelle the truth and erase the look of disdain from her angelic face?

No, he'd stick to his original plan. Gallant courtesies and easygoing charm were the key to overcoming her minor objections to his supposed marital status. With the addition of candlelight, a romantic setting and champagne tomorrow night he couldn't miss, he decided with a complacent smile. Michelle would be his before the week was out, and maybe tonight he could get his first sound sleep. He wished he could talk Glynn into taking an impromptu vacation; he'd never had to deal with a chaperon in residence before, and it was damned inconvenient.

With a groan that was half amusement, half disgust, Alec forced his mind back to his work.

THAT EVENING Michelle looked herself over critically in the cheval mirror. She flipped her thick, single braid over the right shoulder of her periwinkle-blue jumpsuit and turned to the side. The movement turned the sheer metallic knit material from brilliant blue to indigo, causing her to consider changing from the flesh-colored teddy she wore underneath to her navy one. The one she had on now blended so well with her skin she seemed to be wearing nothing at all beneath the thin material. With the gathered cuffs at her wrists and ankles, the otherwise-utilitarian style was enticing.

Yet she knew it wasn't just the color that heightened her complexion and the sparkle in her eyes; it was pure, unadulterated fear. In spite of her anger at Alec—anger that had grown steadily throughout a frustrating afternoon of trying to repair the damage caused by his ex-mistress—Michelle was a mass of nerves. Never before had she blatantly seduced a man.

She was liberated in the sense that she stood up for her rights at work. In a business situation, she was as assertive as her male counterparts. However, none of her three friends' reconditioning had helped her overcome her preliberation upbringing. She'd never called a man for a date or made the first move.

Now she was supposed to walk out of the bedroom and seduce an attractive, extremely experienced man as if she were Salome of the Seven Veils. Not only lead him on, but then laugh in his face. *Oh, Jessica, why aren't you here to give me courage,* she wondered with one last wide-eyed look in the mirror. She walked quickly to the outer door before she lost her nerve, a plastic smile fixed in place.

"Ah, Michelle, you're just in time for a cocktail. I was going to have my second," Alec announced jovially. "Canadian Mist and soda, isn't it?"

"Yes. Lovely," she answered softly, grimacing as her voice cracked. *Oh, Lordie, this is never going to work,* she acknowledged in panic when she took her first real look at her prey. His worn jeans hugged the firm muscles of his thighs and taut, compact buttocks like a second skin as he walked around the end of the bar. Almost apprehensively, she raised her eyes when he turned to face her while mixing her drink, which only intimidated her further.

The soft white cotton jersey of his sweater stretched tightly over his torso and chest as he prepared her drink. The pristine color set off his golden tan and the platinum streaks in his hair. She swallowed a lump in her throat when he walked toward her again.

"Let's have our drinks over by the windows and watch the beginning of the sunset," he said with a slight smile that showed his single dimple.

Michelle nodded quickly, unable to speak under his midnight-blue gaze. She moved swiftly in front of him, hoping her legs would remain steady under her until she reached the couch. She let out a small sigh of relief when she sat down without mishap.

"Your drink, madam," Alec said from above her, silhouetted against the large window. He bowed gracefully from the waist as if he'd been dressed in white tie and tails.

"Thank you," she murmured in return, briefly raising her long lashed eyes to look directly into his. Hastily she lowered them, unable to maintain contact with his direct gaze. Her finger brushed against his, and the resulting electricity caused her almost to drop the glass.

She trucked a leg under her in an attempt to appear casual and relaxed, while surreptitiously watching Alec amble toward the kitchen. The cool glass in her hand felt good against her sweaty palm. Fleetingly she wondered how sexually exciting she'd be breathing into a paper bag to keep from hyperventilating. She shook her head ruefully and took a sip of her drink.

"Is it all right?"

Her eyelashes flew up at Alec's anxious question. His return from the kitchen with a plate of exquisite-looking canapés had been silenced by the thick pile of the taupe carpet. "Oh, yes, just fine."

"Good, that should take care of everything until dinner's ready." He set down the hors d'oeuvres on the nest tables clustered in front of them, and sat next to her, his thigh momentarily brushing against her bent knee. "This is nice. We haven't had much chance to talk over the past few days."

"Mmm, how's the mail-order expansion progressing?" Michelle asked desperately so she wouldn't blurt out, *how come you got tired of your last mistress and she screwed up my accounts program?* Rule number one in man talk, she remembered, was to ask about his work. With every ounce of courage she possessed, she looked straight at him and smiled, tilting her head to the side inquiringly.

"Very well, so far," he responded with an answering smile. Casually he laid his right arm along the back of the couch and crossed his legs, bringing him closer to his companion. He expanded on the problems of adding mail distribution west of the Mississippi.

Michelle replied when necessary, attempting to relax. She allowed his deep voice to wash over her, and tried to appear absorbed in the changing pink-and-lavender sky outside. Although he was talking about business, he seemed preoccupied with her body, curled up next to his. More than once she was aware of his glance dropping below her face. She knew without looking how the vee neck of her jumpsuit caused the material to mold itself to her breasts. He was trying to determine exactly what she wore beneath the material that changed color with each breath she took, which was just as she'd planned.

She wasn't able to meet his intense blue gaze for more than a few moments at a time, but soon realized this was to her advantage. All the feminine ploys she hadn't used in years were beginning to filter through her unease. She continued her shy responses, batting her eyelashes at him. Tentatively she moved her bent leg forward until she made contact with the warm length of his muscular thigh.

"Dinner is ready." Glynn's rough voice broke in on the conversation from the dining area.

"Ah, Glynn, old man, what are we having tonight?" Alec asked without taking his eyes from Michelle. "I skipped lunch today and I'm famished."

"Veal picate, sir, and I took the liberty of chilling a rather nice New York sauterne."

"Just right," Alec assured the older man as he rose to his feet.

Michelle was startled when Alec held out his hand to help her up. She delayed for a minute by placing her glass on the nest tables. Then she surrendered her hand to his larger one and tried to ignore the heat that traveled up her arm and spread through her entire body at the tightening of his grasp. Once she was on her feet he led her to the dinner table, only releasing her hand to seat her.

Unused to so much solicitousness, she wasn't sure where to look. Her glance fell on Glynn, who was looking amused as he lit the long tapers in the center of the table. One of his eyelids lowered almost imperceptibly as he solemnly watched Alec make her comfortable.

"Are we ready to be served now, sir?"

She watched with interest as a flush started at the base of Alec's throat. He sat down abruptly and snapped his napkin in the air before placing it on his lap with great care. This done, he leveled his gaze at the butler. "Yes, now we're ready."

A few minutes later, as Alec tasted his first bite of Glynn's unsurpassed Caesar salad, he wondered if his patience would last through dinner. Suddenly he was getting conflicting signals from Michelle. She wasn't showing any of her former disapproval. Now she was very approachable, endearingly shy and tentative in her responses.

Of course, her choice of attire had sent his blood pressure skyrocketing the moment she'd entered the room. Closer contact didn't lessen her allure. The glittering material that draped her rounded figure tempted him to explore what, if anything, she wore underneath. For the past few days she'd haunted his thoughts merely dressed in her stylishly prim business suits; now, in the clinging blue outfit she had on, she was driving him to the point of madness. The subdued candlelight only added to his frustration.

The meal continued with his mind functioning on two levels. What little he ate of Glynn's expertly prepared food could have been ground glass for all Alec knew, while he and Michelle discussed various places they had visited and enjoyed. He ate automatically and talked casually, all the while fantasizing about peeling the enticing material from Michelle's lush body. By dessert, he'd mentally made love to her three times, unaware that he'd barely eaten half his food and consumed more than a bottle of his best vintage wine.

Michelle's words registered through his erotic daydreams as Glynn entered from the kitchen. "So, I spent two summers in the South of France with *Grand-mère* in order to become a proper lady during college."

Glynn set a cheese-and-fruit board on the table between them, breaking the flow of conversation. Alec relaxed against the back of his chair, purposely slanting her a boyish smile in the hope that it would further his request. "Michelle, I have a favor to ask you."

"Yes, Alec, what is it?"

He noted that her doelike gaze veered from his face once more and she was concentrating on the wineglass in his hand. Her tone was interested, so he pressed on. "Some very close friends of the family are celebrating their fortieth wedding anniversary tomorrow night at the Palmer House. Would you go with me?"

Her demure gaze returned to his face in surprise. He had to restrain a groan as she moistened lips he was aching to taste. Resisting the urge to reach out for her, he sipped his wine. Her gaze didn't waiver for the first time that evening, and he kept his expression as noncommittal as possible. He couldn't allow her to guess how important her answer was, although he sensed she'd accept.

"Yes, that would be fine."

He wanted to jump up from his chair and shout for joy at his easy victory. However, he maintained his rigid control and casually leaned forward to pull a single grape from the cluster on the cheese board. "Good. Why don't we take our wine and dessert over to the window?"

"All right, though I think I'd like to freshen up first." She answered his satisfied grin with a hesitant smile.

He got quickly to his feet, not quite as steady as usual. She stood and turned toward her room. Nothing could have moved him from the spot as he watched her walk the short distance. He sighed when she disappeared through the doorway and he lost his view of her gently swaying hips. He knew he was in for yet another sleepless night. Another night of tossing and turning fitfully, then being wide awake at four in the morning.

"Will there be anything else, sir?"

Alec jumped at the sound of Glynn's voice at his elbow, and splashed wine onto his hand and the tablecloth. "No, Glynn, we'll finish dessert over by the windows."

"Do you want a third bottle of wine?"

At the censorious tone of the manservant's question, Alec looked at the half-full bottle near his place setting. Until that moment he hadn't realized how much had been poured. Michelle's glass was half-full; his was missing only what he'd just spilled.

"No, Glynn, we're fine."

"Yes, sir, that should be enough," he replied, and turned stiffly back toward the kitchen before his scowling employer could reply.

MICHELLE TOOK steadying breaths as she clutched the bathroom countertop. The gentle pats of the cool washcloth hadn't diminished the pink flush of her cheeks or the feverish glint in her eyes. All this, and the man had barely touched her, she thought wildly as she began hyperventilating once more at the idea of what she had to do and with whom.

"Oh, goodness," she gasped with widening eyes as she took in the results of her rapid breaths. The full, rounded curves of her breasts pushed impatiently against the meager barrier of the shimmering blue bodice. The vee neckline opened and closed provocatively to expose her deeply shadowed cleavage above the lace of her teddy. No wonder Alec had been eyeing her like a tasty morsel throughout dinner. He was enjoying the results of her French-cut bra, which more than lifted and separated. That sparkle in his sapphire eyes wasn't from the wine he'd consumed, after all.

"'Goodness has nothing to do with it,'" she quoted dryly to her mirrored image in a poor imitation of Mae West. Her feeble humor didn't help. Oh, how she wished for a little of that lady's sexual repartee at this moment. She had to go back into the living room for round two with her Scandinavian stud armed with about as much sensual savvy as a newborn kitten. And now, every suggestive one-liner of the sultry Mae was repeating itself in her mind, each one only adding to her feelings of inadequacy. She should have drunk more than two glasses of wine.

"Damn you, Fred, for even suggesting I seduce your brother," she muttered, turning resolutely toward the door. To stop the taunting refrain of the irreverent Mae in her subconscious, she concentrated on the painstaking—and fruitless—attempt to repair her computer program that afternoon. Repairs made necessary by Alec's amorous whims. Both she and Alec were paying for his capricious love life. If even his sister, who wasn't aware of the newest problem, thought he deserved a lesson for his lies, then Michelle had to persevere.

Her first sight of Alec, and his appreciative smile, made her feel instantly like a Christian being thrown to a hungry lion.

"*Mademoiselle*, let me fulfill your every wish," he announced with a sweeping bow from the waist. He kept his wineglass from tilting in the hand he extended with a flourish. He seated her with a great display of courtliness, then turned to the food on the low table in front of them.

She tried not to watch the play of his shoulder muscles beneath his sweater as he filled a plate with a selection of fruit and cheeses. This was difficult, since he was directly at eye level and so temptingly close to her touch. She looked around for any distraction.

The sun had set during her absence, and the city was blanketed in darkness. Glittering chains of lights twinkled at her feet. A single lamp had been turned on behind the bar, giving off a soft glow, muted classical music played in the background. The atmosphere seemed to envelop her like a cocoon. Michelle was startled when the couch dipped under Alec's weight as he sat beside her.

He handed her her replenished glass and bent forward to retrieve his own. Then he sat back with a gratifying sign, balancing a single plate on his leg. "We'll share a plate and save Glynn some cleanup time in the kitchen."

Michelle nodded mutely, cowardly blocking out the sight of his conspiratorial smile and the blue flame of his eyes by lowering her eyelashes. Immediately she regretted the action. Her line of vision was narrowed to his taut, denim-encased thigh that balanced their shared dessert. She took a hearty swallow of wine, hoping it might cool the heat being transferred from his hard thigh to her leg.

"Can I tempt *mademoiselle*?"

Michelle's eyes flew to meet his smoldering gaze. "A slice of apple, or perhaps a grape?" Alec continued.

"Please, peel me a grape," she drawled huskily. Alec couldn't know that the reason she replied in so throaty and suggestive a tone was that she'd been trying to swallow her tongue.

His hungry eyes momentarily widened in surprise before he broke into a grin that deepened his attractive dimple. Michelle's heart slammed against her rib cage in an erratic tattoo. Her lion had gone from hungry to ravenous.

"I have a much better idea," he said, quickly moving to place his glass and the plate of food on the nest tables. This done, he removed her glass from her suddenly lifeless fingers and turned it deliberately. Slowly he brought the glass to his lips at the exact spot on the rim where she had drank moments earlier. He drained the glass of the wine that remained and placed it, empty, on the table, his eyes never leaving her face.

She watched apprehensively as he picked up the cluster of plump, wine-red grapes by the stem. Swallowing nervously, she knew it would be impossible for her to consume a single one.

"We'll eat them in the grand style of ancient Rome."

She froze, staring at him in astonishment. He was reading her mind and going in for the kill. Then she chided herself for her wild flight of fancy. The man was merely practising a very polished seduction, although her rationalizing was no more comfort to her than her earlier imagery had been.

"I can see *mademoiselle* is confused," Alec said with a slight chuckle, misinterpreting her frown. He settled himself closer to her, resting his arm behind her along the back of the couch. "Let me demonstrate. It's really quite simple."

In fascination she watched him tilt back his head and hold the grapes suspended over his mouth. When his strong white teeth closed over one dangling grape, she felt a tremor of excitement shoot up her spine at the thought of him nibbling as tenderly on her skin.

"Okay? You try it."

She shook her head, hoping to avert any further danger, but her reluctance only seemed to make him more determined.

He smiled in tolerant understanding as his arm snaked around her shoulders to guide her toward the back of the couch. Once she was settled to his satisfaction in the cradle of his arm and shoulder, he leaned over to whisper in her ear, "It's very easy, *ma petite*, just watch the bottom grape. Take it between your teeth and trap it with your tongue, then pull."

He wasn't to be denied the silly game, she decided, watching defenselessly as he lowered the cluster of grapes to her mouth. She was distracted by the feel of his taut chest muscles as they pressed intimately against her side. She'd reached out in panic, and only now realized she was clutching the hard sinew of his thigh. Her entire body was on fire, and she was aware of every inch of the devastating man holding her. The smooth fruit brushed her lips. Instinctively she opened her mouth to let him lower the fruit inside. Her eyes locked with his, mere inches away as she automatically followed his instructions by wrapping her tongue around the small sphere.

She felt his groan begin deep in his chest and rumble upward against her shoulder before the low sound escaped his parted lips. Lost in the stormy blue sea of his gaze, she chewed the grape and swallowed without being aware of her actions. He didn't move. The soft, enticing sound of violins and French horns surrounded them. Nervously Michelle wet her dry lips with the tip of her tongue.

The tiny, hesitant movement brought Alec's mesmerizing gaze to her moistened mouth. "Oh, Lord, sweetheart, I have to taste you. Now."

The husky words were barely spoken before his lips met hers. It wasn't the gentle, tentative touch of a first kiss. He was hungry and demanding as his tongue stabbed into the sweet interior of her mouth. He used his lips and teeth to satisfy his starvation. Michelle had never experienced anything as rough or exciting. Her body ignited under his demanding hands. She reached out, pulling Alec closer into her embrace to sate her own appetite.

Time became an unreal measurement as their wild embrace continued. There was only the sound of their ragged breathing and moans of approval with each new caress. The music swelled and Michelle experienced feelings of passion and desire totally new to her. When Alec surrendered possession of her mouth to travel down her throat with kisses, she thought the fire in her blood would consume her. Never had she imagined being so out of control. Yet it didn't frighten her. She only ached for more.

She cried out in anticipation as his blunt fingers discovered the hidden clasp of her jumpsuit at her waist. In an erotic daze, she waited for him to remove the confining clothing from her aching breasts. She wanted to be free, open to his pleasure.

Slowly, almost reverently, Alec pulled away the shimmering material that had fascinated him all evening. With hazy detachment, Michelle realized they were now lying side by side on the couch. She reached out for Alec, anxious to renew the delight of his embrace, which had caused the smoldering warmth in her abdomen. However, his strong hands manacled her wrists before she could touch him.

Alec secured Michelle's searching hands against the cushions on either side of her shoulders and rolled her beneath him. He had to regain his reason. Since the moment he'd claimed her intoxicating lips, he'd been totally out of control. Never in his life had he felt such a consuming need.

Through desire-glazed eyes he allowed himself a long, lingering look at her half-bare body. The plunging vee of the camisole was bordered in a wide band of lace that left little to his imagination. Lace and the sheerest bra he'd ever seen didn't hide her creamy white breasts. He resisted the urge to taste the light dusting of freckles over her breastbone, knowing it would only tempt him to seek out the flavor of her tawny pink nipples.

"We have to slow down, love," he whispered hoarsely, catching his breath sharply as she moved beneath him. She murmured an entreating sound when her movements pressed his arousal into the soft swell of her stomach.

He released his hold on one of her wrists. In surprise he noticed his hand was trembling as he raised it to brush back the feathery wisps of hair at her temple. Her dishabille clouded his wine-befuddled brain even more.

"Sweetheart, we need to slow down," he repeated, cursing himself for having drunk so much and attacking her like an untried adolescent. Michelle was intoxicating enough without drugs. "I want to savor our first time together."

"Kiss me, Alec," she murmured in a seductive tone, nuzzling her cheek into his palm. Her deep brown eyes sparkled an invitation from beneath half-closed eyelids.

He shut his eyes to block the sight of her parted lips, swollen from his kisses. A more disturbing image formed in his mind: the sight of Michelle flushed in the aftermath of a night's loving, tumbled amid the sheets of his bed in the first light of morning. He fought for control, the effort draining his energy and weakening his resolve.

Soft, tapered fingers moved stealthily beneath his sweater. He opened his eyes abruptly, and was met by Michelle's alluringly sweet smile. He could feel his blood pounding against his temples as he strove to ignore the burning heat where she'd caressed his ribs before moving on in feathery touches to the sensitive skin of his back. Swiftly he rolled to his side, trapping her hand between his back and the couch. He still retained possession of her other hand, and placed it over his rapidly beating heart.

"One kiss, Alec," she bargained, her expression slightly hurt.

He gave in to her request, relaxing slightly. The strain of resisting was affecting his entire body. A feeling of lethargy overrode his desire, while his reasoning was becoming fuzzy. It seemed to take great effort to move his head the few inches forward. When he brushed his lips lightly over Michelle's, his body and mind were sending him conflicting signals.

One told him to rest and move slowly, while the other was impatient to make love to the soft, lovely woman in his arms. He compromised by trailing his lips downward over the silken skin of her cheek to the inviting curve at the base of her neck. Her sigh of disappointment changed to a murmur of approval as he teased the sensitive area of her collarbone with gentle kisses.

"So soft, so soft," he whispered, resting his head against the cushion of her shoulder. Her heady scent of roses and garden flowers filled his overstimulated brain as he tried matching the aroma with the taste of her skin. He closed his eyes to savor her assault on his senses.

"Alec?" Michelle's tentative inquiry a few minutes later was answered by the woffling sound of a masculine snore.

5

HE WAS ASLEEP! Michelle was stunned. She wasn't sure whether to laugh or scream or cry as Alec shifted and snuggled his head more comfortably against her breasts. Once the initial shock had passed, she realized relief was the feeling that dominated all others. Relief that Alec's wine consumption had saved her from being caught in her own trap.

Tonight proved her apprehensions were well founded, but for the wrong reasons. It wasn't her lack of experience that was dangerous; the real peril was her response to Alec's lovemaking. Once he'd touched her she'd been ensnared by the magic he created. She'd willingly followed his lead. Forgotten were his lies about being married, his callous treatment of Magda and the unpleasant aftermath that had destroyed her own work.

On one level she'd acknowledged the physical chemistry between them, but had allowed her anger and disapproval of the man to overshadow the fact. After tonight she couldn't deny that Alec possessed a unique ability to ignite her passionate nature. Even the intimacy she'd shared with Stuart paled in comparison. With a single kiss Alec could make her forget everything, including her own name. All she'd wanted was to consummate their explosive lovemaking.

Her renegade thoughts rekindled the longing in her unsatisfied body. Alec stirred once more, draping his leg over her thigh. She knew she should be angry, but instead she was having difficulty in suppressing her laughter. Her Scandinavian stud had no head for wine. Dale Robeson would be amazed to discover just how innocently the experienced Alec had slept with her—twice. Then she grimaced. She hoped no one at Lindfors House would ever know, since it didn't say much for her appeal, no matter how much wine Alec had drank or the quality of the vintage. Although telling Jessica could possibly make her brother's life miserable for years.

A perverse idea took shape in her mind that would fall into Jessica's plans to teach Alec a lesson and allow Michelle the upper hand. Alec would have more than a hangover to worry about in the morning. She moved cautiously under his deadweight to see just how unconscious her would-be lover was, or if he was merely playing possum. When her experimental movements didn't seem to bother him, she became bolder. Slipping her free hand from his relaxed grip, she reached behind her to grasp the edge of one of the nest tables. Slowly she edged her lower half off the couch, allowing Alec's leg to come gradually to rest on the cushion.

Her left arm and shoulder were still trapped beneath Alec's solid body. She sat for a minute, considering her next move. Awkwardly she brought up her knees and exerted pressure on the nest table with her free hand to raise her hips from the carpet. Although lopsided with her arm imprisoned, she managed to maneuver herself into a kneeling position. She hesitated only once—when her foot bumped the table leg, causing their wineglasses to clink. However, the bell-like echo of fine crystal in the quiet of the room had no effect on the slumbering Alec.

She smiled in anticipation as she gradually pulled her numb arm from its warm prison. Alec grumbled slightly but remained asleep. When she was free, Michelle scrambled to her feet and planned her next move while she waited for her circulation to return. She may have been distracted from her purpose by Alec's drugging kisses, but his falling asleep was an unforeseen stroke of good luck. What she was about to do would certainly give Mr. Love-'em-and-leave-'em Lindfors some unsettling moments, if she could pull it off.

Alec moved again, rolling onto his back, one arm flung over the back of the couch.

"Perfect, just perfect," Michelle whispered, allowing her anticipatory grin to widen as she refastened her jumpsuit. With a deep breath she bent to her task.

First she slipped off his loafers, mouthing a silent thank-you to Don Johnson—Alec wasn't wearing socks. Then she moved back to his head, amazed by how innocent and defenseless he looked in sleep. Cautiously she rolled his sweater up over the firm muscles of his abdomen and the gorgeous expanse of his chest, careful to avoid touching his mat of golden hair. A shiver of delight tiptoed up her spine as she remembered the feel of his well-toned body pressing hers into the cushions where he now lay. With deadly slow movements she maneuvered his limp arms out of the sleeves of the soft, white material. The vee neck of his sweater allowed her to slip it over his head with little difficulty.

She flung the garment haphazardly over her shoulder in a show of bravado she didn't quite feel. His jeans were next. On the count of ten, she tentatively reached for the snap and zipper with unsteady fingers. When she opened both fastenings, she froze momentarily, until she saw a slight band of green elastic peeking from beneath the opening. She hadn't considered that he might be naked underneath his jeans; his bare chest was intimidating enough. She didn't think there was anything sexier than an attractive man stripped to a pair of body-hugging jeans.

Her eyes focused on the back of the couch—and trusting her peripheral vision—she worked at moving the soft denim down his lean hips. He cooperated beautifully by moving at just the right moment, but a quick glance at his slumbering face assured her he was still asleep. The task of removing his jeans from each muscular leg was child's play. Fleetingly she wondered how often Glynn performed this chore with more charitable motives when Alec had indulged too much.

She flung the denim pants aside in the same manner as his sweater. Her most ambitious feat still lay ahead—removing the almost unnecessary scrap of dark green cotton briefs that molded his very male anatomy. For a moment she considered leaving him as he was, but knew all the while that her plan would be more effective if he were completely nude.

"You've seen the man naked before, so get to it," she muttered under her breath with no conviction at all. The brief glimpse of his nude body had almost unhinged her the first time. She had to admit he was impressively built.

He moved onto his side again, and Michelle decided it was now or never. She took a deep breath and went back to work. She focused on the golden down that covered his upper thighs and she wished she could do this with her eyes shut, but one false move could bring Alec awake. It took less than a minute, which seemed like an eternity. She didn't realize she was holding her breath until her lungs began to burn.

She released her breath in a whoosh as Alec turned onto his stomach, and allowed herself a satisfying look at her success while twirling his undergarment on her hand.

"And I'm going to bed alone," she mused softly, studying Alec, superbly naked and alone on the couch.

Resisting the impulse to give him a departing pat on his inviting buttocks, she hurried off to her room. While she undressed, she couldn't help but think that her plan needed a finishing touch. The cluster of grapes draped over his ear was out of the question. What else would give Alec second thoughts about tonight? When she picked up her discarded clothes, she knew exactly what would do it. She dropped the pile of clothing and gave the sash of her kimono a decisive tug.

An impish grin spread over her face as she crept back to the quiet living room. He hadn't moved an inch, but he did have a rather silly smile on his face. Hurriedly she arranged her sheer bra on the floor beneath the nest table nearest his head. When she straightened she paused for a moment at an unfamiliar sound. No other noise followed, so she dismissed it as just the furniture settling for the night and quickly went back to her room. She knew it was too late to reconsider; there was no way she could possible dress him again. Her plan was set in motion.

SOMETHING WAS TICKLING his nose, Alec realized without opening his eyes. He didn't want to move. Besides, his eyelids felt as if they weighed about forty pounds apiece. The tickling didn't stop. With great effort he raised his hand to capture the instrument of his torture. Instead of the silken strawberry-blond hair he'd imagined, his hand closed around textured material.

He managed the Herculean effort of opening his eyes. What looked like the belt to his cranberry velour robe was in his palm. His gaze followed the taut material, which rose perpendicular from his fingers to the large, beefy hand that held it suspended over him.

"Did we enjoy ourselves?"

Alec blinked, hoping it would help clear his head. This wasn't making any sense. Where was Michelle? She'd been snuggling up against him just before the tickling had begun. He was sure she'd been tickling him with the tip of her thick braid. Next time he'd make love to her with her hair unbound, wrapping himself in the warm honeyed fire. *The next time? What had happened to this time?*

"Glynn, what time is it?" The words came out in a thick, guttural voice. He wasn't surprised; his tongue felt as if it had ballooned to three times its normal size and been given a thick coat of paint.

"Too late," the older man answered, adding after a brief pause, "about midnight."

"What?" At the surprising answer, Alec bolted upright. Only three hours had passed since they'd finished dinner. He regretted the precipitous movement instantly. Sharp pain lanced the base of his skull and set up a throbbing in his temples. He dropped his legs over the side of the couch, bringing his hands up to clasp his aching head. When his elbows came to rest on his thighs, naked skin met naked skin. Something must have happened, or else why wasn't he dressed? An even more urgent question flashed into his mind. Why wasn't he in his own bed with Michelle beside him?

"I said it's about midnight," Glynn repeated loudly, not seeming to care about his employer's physical condition.

Alec wanted to shake his head to clear its cotton-wool stuffing, but knew that would be painful. Instead he continued to support the intolerable weight of his head in his hands. Slowly he cocked his head until the towering Glynn came into his line of vision. Immediately he regretted the action.

Glynn's granite-hewn features were thrown into relief by the lamp that had been turned on at the end of the couch. Although his face showed no animation, his gray eyes were sparkling very suspiciously, from Alec's jaundiced viewpoint. There was more to Glynn's suppressed emotion than superiority at being sober and clearheaded. The older man had yet to call him by name or tack on the obligatory "sir." Alec knew that didn't bode well for their conversation.

He didn't bother to move when Glynn began collecting the scattered remnants of his clothing. Abstractly he wondered how his sweater had ended up three feet away against the windows. "Why are you up?"

Glynn continued to shake out the white sweater and answered without turning to look at his employer. "I thought I heard a noise earlier."

"I see." He didn't but thought it would be prudent not to pursue the matter any further. Gingerly he moved his hands over his face in a scrubbing motion. When that had little effect in clearing his head, he rubbed his eyes with the heels of his hands. Although not overly modest, he felt uncomfortable at the thought of standing up stark naked in front of Glynn. Most of all he didn't want to hear Glynn's comments on the fact.

"Here, before you catch a chill," came the other man's gravelly voice over his shoulder just seconds before soft cranberry-colored material enveloped Alec's head.

Very carefully Alec pulled the garment off his aching head. He awkwardly put on his robe while still seated. Out of the corner of his eye he saw the belt where Glynn had dropped it. Holding his head very still, he leaned to the side and stretched out his arm. He grunted in triumph when his hand closed over the cloth, but when he straightened he held an extremely feminine bit of clothing.

"Very fetching, sir," Glynn offered in a tone as dry as sandpaper.

Alec tore his fascinated gaze from Michelle's sheer bra and glared at the manservant. "Is there something you'd like to say, Homer?"

"It's just that you hadn't informed me of this change in style."

Alec realized he held in his hand the evidence of having seduced Michelle, and didn't remember a blessed thing about it. What was even worse, he was getting the impression Glynn knew more than he did.

"Will there be anything else before I retire? Perhaps a little hair of the dog, or a pair of panty hose or a brain transplant?"

"You're fired, Homer," Alec bit out.

"Oh, very good. A new record," Glynn replied cheerfully, then sauntered toward the kitchen with Alec's clothes. "You've never fired me twice within the same week."

Alec muttered a few choice words under his breath. Then his attention was absorbed once more by the scrap of lace and satin in his hand. He had a clear vision of Michelle's soft body beneath his with only this and her lace camisole covering her voluptuous curves. The only other memory was his head resting on the bountiful softness of her breasts, her perfume filling his senses. The proof that it wasn't a dream was in his hand. He just didn't know how much was real and how much was fantasy.

For the present he had to concentrate on standing up and walking to his bedroom. Moving slowly so he wouldn't jar his head, he managed the distance in ten minutes. He felt foolishly disappointed that there wasn't a shapely redhead in his bed. That meant that whatever he'd done, Michelle had gone to her own room.

"Argh!" he sputtered minutes later under the ice-cold rush of the shower. Although the Spartan treatment finally brought him fully awake, it had no effect on his memory. He had a clear vision of dinner as he toweled himself dry with controlled movements—Michelle's sweet face glowing in soft candlelight, her thick braid draped over her shoulder. He remembered wanting to unwind her thick, molten rope of hair and bury himself in the soft, silky tresses.

"Oh, Lord, why did I drink so much?" he questioned his tousled, blurry-eyed reflection in the bathroom mirror. He was almost afraid to discover the answer. There was only one other occasion on which he'd felt this lousy—the night his father had died. That night he'd gone to Glynn to talk, and they'd gotten blind, staring drunk.

He shuffled to his bed and sat dejectedly on the edge. His father's company was now in jeopardy from a mistake in judgment over one woman, and the woman who'd caused him to drink so much on an empty stomach had the means with which to resolve the crisis that had resulted. So where did he go from here, he wondered dispiritedly.

He lay down without bothering to remove the bedspread, knowing he wouldn't be sleeping. *This must be a mid-life crisis,* he decided. The thought of encroaching middle age seemed more comforting than making a fool of himself over a woman. Of course, he very likely had done just that tonight, he reflected grimly as he clasped his hands behind his head.

When he closed his eyes to concentrate, the room went into a tailspin. Abruptly he opened them again, still trying to separate reality and fantasy. Dinner was real, although he'd imagined a number of erotic scenes while they ate. Taking dessert over to the couch was real, the first hungry kisses they'd exchanged had been real. His imagination couldn't have created the amazing physical reactions he recalled.

Michelle haunted his thoughts like no other woman in his life, and had from the moment she'd arrived. He'd tried to analyze his emotions with little success. Tonight, for example, when she'd first entered the room

he'd had a sense of déjà vu. However, he dismissed it
now as he had then. He was a practical man. It was
simply a surge of desire for an attractive woman.

He swore heatedly and at length. Nothing was clear.
All his fantasies and what could have happened
merged. The more he tried to remember, the more his
head hurt. There was no solution, unless he asked the
one person who knew.

Finally he gave up. Tomorrow he had to face Michelle without having any idea of what had happened.
That meant he'd need to devise a plan. He had to use
every ounce of his charm and experience with women
to discover what they had done tonight, without her
guessing the truth.

"Sure, Lindfors, and pigs can fly."

"HOLD THE ELEVATOR, please."

Alec opened his eyes at the sound of the familiar female voice he'd last heard some twelve hours ago. He
straightened in anticipation from where he was leaning against the back wall of the car. By some stroke of
luck he was going to meet Michelle the minute he arrived at work. Unfortunately it would also be in a
crowded elevator at lunchtime.

She was framed in the opening, flushed and out of
breath. Her arms were filled with packages, and a large
dress box swung from one hand. When she gave the
man who held open the door a grateful smile and offered her thanks, Alec envied him. She stepped back
into the front corner, momentarily blocked from Alec's
view.

He moved to bring her back into his line of vision,
appreciatively scanning her white linen suit and cherry-

red blouse. That morning he'd stayed in his room until she'd left. He hadn't been in any condition at that point to discuss their evening together. With a humorless smile, he thought he should have waited until Glynn had left, too.

Idly he counted twelve people in the elevator, wishing they'd all disappear. The car seemed to be stopping at every floor, but the number of occupants remained constant as new arrivals replaced those departing. At each stop he edged closer to Michelle.

Unexpectedly she turned her head, almost as if she sensed his presence. He froze under the spell of her startled brown eyes. Her glossy red lips trembled in a tentative smile, and she lowered her thick lashes. A rosy flush began to rise from the open collar of her blouse. Now he was sure they'd made love last night.

He relaxed his tense muscles. A protective feeling washed over him and without further hesitation he stepped confidently around the people who stood between them.

"Hello," he said gently, placing his hand on the wall next to her, blocking out the others around them. "I missed you this morning."

Her dark lashes swept upward to disclose her searching gaze. He had to stifle a groan as the tip of her tongue appeared and she delicately wet her lips. "Hello, Alec."

Her husky whisper caused a shaft of desire to lance through him. He noticed her arm tighten around the packages she clutched against her breasts. Her blush deepened as she glanced nervously to the side.

"It's all right, darling," he assured her, bending his head to speak directly into her ear. "Tomorrow's Saturday and we can sleep in."

Her head came up suddenly, making it necessary for him to draw back. Something flashed in her eyes, causing them to deepen to an obsidian hue. Then her lashes hid them from sight as an entrancing secret smile curved her lips.

"Perhaps you're right," she answered in a husky drawl. "We'll just have to see if tonight is like last night."

Alec cocked his head, trying to interpret her meaning. Her shyness was turning to provocative teasing. This new side of her personality intrigued as well as frustrated him. Although he was now positive they'd made love, he still couldn't remember any details and her tantalizing comments held no clues.

"Sweetheart . . ." he began in an undertone.

"*Ma petite* was much more romantic," she interrupted gently, giving him a wicked sidelong glance from beneath her lashes.

He chuckled knowingly, in spite of the fact he had no idea what she was talking about. They'd talked about her trips to France to visit her grandmother at dinner, but when had he translated endearments with his limited French?

"*Ma petite* . . ." he began, but again was cut off by a cheerful voice from the entrance to the elevator. Lew Rizzo sidestepped one person and jostled another before he stopped next to them. "Hi, guys."

Alec choked back an expletive. Although he knew he couldn't fire the kid for getting on the elevator, when he saw Michelle's warm smile for the younger man, he considered it.

"Michelle, you should've come over to Grant Park. There was a terrific jazz combo. Shopping couldn't have been that much fun."

"You never know, sweetie." She laughed and wiggled her eyebrows while moving a step away from Alec. "I have a special engagement tonight."

"Friday night and time to howl, huh?"

"Perhaps," she returned with a slow suggestive smile. Alec wasn't sure, but he thought she winked at him.

"So, Alec, how 'bout you? Are you staying in town or heading home to Lake Forest?" Lew asked innocently, then continued to make his boss regret his policy of being friendly and open with his staff. "Someday I'm going to have an apartment in town and a house in the suburbs."

Alec was considering murdering Lew Rizzo until he looked at Michelle. She wasn't angry at the discovery that he had another home. In fact, she was downright amused. Her eyes were dancing with suppressed laughter, and she caught her lower lip in her teeth to stop the smile that trembled at the corners of her mouth.

I can murder Lew and plead temporary insanity, he thought wildly as they both waited for his answer. He was given a reprieve by the muted ding of the elevator bell and the soft whoosh of the opening doors.

"Well, here we are back at the old grindstone," Lew quipped, and stepped back to allow Michelle to precede him out of the elevator.

Alec followed them down the hallway, ignoring the duo's conversation. His brain was still functioning at half speed, but he knew choking the life out of Lew was out of the question. He knew he couldn't confront Michelle in the office, either.

He sighed resignedly just as Lew and Michelle disappeared through the office entrance. The disclosure of last night's secrets would have to wait until later, when there was candlelight, music and champagne—at least, champagne for Michelle, he amended hastily. He realized the irony of the fact that this was the same plan he'd devised the day before.

Well, he thought philosophically as he entered the office, *apparently it worked last night. At least, I think it did.*

He shoved his hands into his pockets and barely grunted in response to Katrin's greeting.

"THE AUDACITY of the man," Michelle grumbled, punctuating each word by tossing down her packages one by one. The anger she'd contained in the elevator and while getting rid of Lew finally spilled forth. "He didn't even hesitate. It was right past Go, collect two hundred dollars and yes, sir, she's easy, so let's do it again."

"'Tomorrow's Saturday,'" she mimicked as she flung herself into the swivel chair behind the desk. "Oh, that man's ego must be the size of the Sears Tower." She twirled the chair around to relieve some of her frustrations. About halfway through the spin an image of Alec's nude body flashed through her mind. Immediately an involuntary chuckle escaped her lips. "Michelle Henrietta Moens, you have a filthy mind, and you certainly didn't do a thing to make Alec think you hadn't slept with him."

She put out her foot to stop the chair and sighed. Grudgingly she admitted Alec's oversize ego had helped her in those first agonizing minutes in the elevator. When she'd gotten back to work at lunchtime, she'd still been on that special high that comes from buying beautiful clothes.

The day had started wonderfully, too, with a very affable Glynn announcing Alec would be late going to work. She'd practically walked on air to the office. A few times during the morning she'd had momentary qualms about what she'd done, bracing herself for Alec's appearance at any moment, but her cheerful mood had reasserted itself when she'd learned Alec still hadn't made an appearance by lunchtime. She'd gone off then to make a number of State Street merchants very happy in the next hour.

She'd found the dress almost immediately. It was a stylized Edwardian design of chiffon and silk char-meuse that no lady of that era would have dared wear in public. From the puffed sleeves to the handkerchief hemline, it was quite demure, but sheer chiffon cov ered her shoulders and the upper swells of her breasts, culminating in a ruffle at her throat.

Michelle made her next purchase, following her French grandmother's rule that no woman's outfit was complete without the perfect intimate apparel. She carefully selected an ecru lace *bustier* and taupe satin bikini panties.

A few more purchases finished off the ensemble that would turn Alec into a blithering idiot. Glitter for her hair, stiletto sandals and a sheer ivory cashmere shawl were added to her feminine arsenal. She'd returned to the Lindfors House office building with only minutes to spare. The shock of seeing the victim of her shopping spree standing at the back of the elevator paralyzed her for a few precious seconds. Then a devious streak in her nature surfaced that she'd never known she possessed.

While Alec moved slowly toward her, she'd rapidly calculated her next move. She'd allowed him to take the initiative, then fallen back on her demure, fluttering-eyelash routine, and the egotistical stud had taken the bait. By immediately assuming they'd made love, he'd also given her the incentive of anger to play the tease.

Michelle chuckled again as she looked over the packages that contained enough feminine armament to melt an iceberg, let alone a man with a low boiling point such as Alec. Jessica would be amazed at the monster she'd created with her dare of teaching her brother a lesson. After Michelle was finished with Alec, he'd probably consider becoming a monk.

For the rest of the afternoon Michelle found herself giggling at odd moments and the time seemed to drag. Yet she knew she'd never felt so alive, anticipating the evening ahead with Alec.

"THANKS, BUT, NO. I'm going to sit this one out," Michelle said with a gracious smile to her would-be dance partner a few hours later. She sat down at the table for two, grateful to rest her aching feet. It seemed as if she'd danced with every man at the Wilkins' party since their arrival an hour earlier.

"Well, hello. Have we met before?"

Alec's sarcastic words from the seat next to her made Michelle pause for a second before taking a refreshing sip of ice water. Carefully she set down the stemmed glass and turned to study his face. He no longer had the glazed look that had appeared the moment she'd removed her shawl.

So far everything had gone according to her plan. She'd stayed in her room until just minutes before it was time to leave. By draping her shawl backward, she'd concealed the revealing bodice of her dress. Alec's appreciative smile when she entered the living room had heightened her expectations and helped her to deal with the impact of his nonchalant elegance.

When they'd arrived at the hotel, Alec had gallantly extended a hand to help her out of the taxi. As she'd shifted to place her feet on the pavement, the wind had rearranged the delicate material of her skirt. The sudden rush of air had caught her hem, baring one leg to Alec's interested gaze. His attentive smile momentarily widened to a lecherous grin at the unexpected sight of a lace garter and bare flesh above her ivory stockings.

Minutes later, his expression had been one of stupefaction when Michelle had removed the concealing cashmere with a flourish. He wasn't alone; a number of men's eyes had been drawn to the enticing dress. Those who knew Alec had quickly come to the table for an introduction. For the past hour she'd barely had time to exchange more than three words with her escort. Every time she settled in her chair for more than a minute yet another new dance partner would appear.

Now, at the look on Alec's face, she suppressed a smile. There was no mistaking his expression: he was sulking. She knew he hadn't moved since they'd arrived, except to signal a waiter to replenish his club soda. All that was missing was thrusting out his lower lip.

"Hello yourself, handsome stranger," she answered with a flirtatious smile. All the flattering attention from Alec's friends had given her the daring she needed to overcome his dark mood. She reached over to flick his black bow tie. When his sullen look remained, she cupped her chin in her palm to assess the situation. Alec still didn't respond when she gave him a saucy wink, although his melancholy gaze never left her face.

Her self-assurance began to waiver under his un-flinching regard. *Damn the man, they're his friends. I only danced with them to be sociable.* Did he expect her to sit there and glare at him all night?

"Wanna dance, mister?" The words sprang out before she had a chance to think, but she got to her feet expectantly just the same.

He didn't answer except to kick back his chair and stand next to her. He hesitated a moment, then took her hand to lead her to the dance floor, where he clamped his hands at her waist, forcing her to place her palms against his ruffled shirt to keep her balance when he began to dance.

This is ridiculous. She looked solemnly at her partner's stern face, masking her rebellious thoughts. *He's not going to ruin my evening.*

She thought for a second. The tactic that flitted through her mind wasn't the best alternative, but it was the only one that was feasible at the moment.

She let one hand slide up the crisp white ruffles of his shirt to the edge of his collar. Resisting the urge to throttle him, she traced the tanned skin of his neck. Rising slightly on tiptoe, she raised her lips until she could feel his warm breath against them. She smiled, and an uncertain, watchful look came into his eyes.

"Now if sugah is gonna pout all evenin', yo'r jest gonna have ta stick out yo lowah lip in the propah mannah," she drawled in a syrupy imitation of her next-door-neighbor in Atlanta. To emphasize the point, she grazed his lower lip with the pad of her thumb. At first she thought her nonsense would have no effect—proving she was an abysmal failure as a flirt—but then she felt his lip quiver slightly.

"That is the worst Southern accent I've ever heard," he accused with a chuckle, hugging her closer to his chest. His warm hands roamed over her supple back to hold her in place. Then his whole body stiffened. "What do you have on under this? A corset?"

His incredulous look was almost comical, but Michelle didn't laugh. She could feel the heated flush rapidly coloring her skin.

"Um, not exactly," she started hesitantly. *Lord, why did I ask him to dance? I should've left him there sulking.* "It's called a *bustier*, just lace, a few stays and garters. It goes with my dress sort of."

"Sort of?" Alec parroted hoarsely, and swallowed rapidly. His eyes darkened as he avidly inspected the diaphanous material that enhanced rather than detracted from the alluring swell of her breasts. Michelle recognized the same dazed expression from earlier this evening.

"Alec, are you all right?"

Closing his eyes, he slowly moved his head from side to side. However, moments later his lashes rose to reveal a glimmer of amusement in the depths of his eyes, and a half smile quirked his perfectly chiseled lips.

"Wearing the most seductively gorgeous dress I've ever seen, you ask me if I'm all right? Not to mention that tantalizing glimpse of your lace garter you gave me just before you ignored me for every other man in the place." He paused to take a deep breath and then continued. "Now you blithely tell me you're wearing lingerie straight from the cover of an erotic French novel. Am I all right?"

"But, Alec, you asked—"

"You're either the most wicked or the most honestly naive woman I've ever met. Or perhaps you're an imp of the Devil, come to make me pay for my past sins."

She didn't even need the telltale heat under her skin to tell her she was blushing once more. This time it was from guilt. His joking remark was too near the truth; he *was* paying for his past sins, along with Stuart's and all the other men who'd lied for the sake of their pleasure and convenience. She didn't know where to look, positive her distress was apparent in her expression. The orchestra seemed to take pity on her at the moment, for the medley of ballads came to an end. Quickly she stepped out of his embrace.

Her reprieve was short-lived. Alec was at her side as she walked back to their table, his arm possessively around her shoulders. He didn't release her when they reached their destination. Keeping her securely tucked against his side, he picked up her purse and shawl. She dared a peek at his face. He was glaring at one of her former partners, who'd made the mistake of approaching them at that moment.

"I think we've been here long enough to properly represent the family," Alec explained while turning her in the direction of the door. "It's time we paid a visit to your favorite view of the city."

"But, Alec, you've barely spoken to the Wilkins, just in the receiving line when we came in," she protested as he guided her down the shallow steps to the lobby. Wishing the Oriental carpet would suddenly open and swallow her as they crossed the cavernous room, she trotted to keep up with his purposeful strides. All her courage and bravado of the afternoon and early evening evaporating the minute they left behind the safety of the crowded party.

"We only needed to make an appearance. John was a business friend of my father's and Mother occasionally plays bridge with Gina," Alec said affably just as they came to the escalator leading to the street level. He positioned Michelle in front of him and let his hands rest lightly on her shoulders as they descended. "I gave them the family's congratulations, and Mother sent an expensive gift from Tokyo when her cruise ship stopped there, and that's that. Now we'll take time for ourselves where there won't be any more interruptions."

6

MICHELLE BARELY NOTICED the dimly lit display windows of the closed arcade shops; her sights were focused on the revolving door and her thoughts on the taxi lurking out there somewhere that would take her to her doom. What she really wanted was to run as fast as she could in the opposite direction, anyplace away from the excitement of Alec Lindfors. She knew her courage was almost completely gone.

She called herself a coward and a fool, thinking back to her cocky predictions of what this night would bring. Numbly she allowed Alec to drape her shawl around her shoulders to shield her from the slight chill of the evening air. She tried to ignore the warm protection of his arm while they waited for a cab. However, she couldn't mask her surprise when he raised her hand gently and kissed the inside of her wrist before handing her into the car.

His presence seemed to dominate the dark confines of the back seat and it took great strength of will for her to keep from burrowing into the corner. Instead she tried to act as nonchalant as possible, although she realized that she couldn't remember a single thing she'd planned to do when they got back to Alec's apartment. Every ounce of self-confidence seemed to have been carried off by the night breeze. She jumped when Alec turned toward her and placed his hand over hers, which was clenching the tail of her shawl in a death grip.

All I have to do is hang on for another half hour, Michelle cautioned herself as Alec laid his free arm around her shoulders with practiced ease. But when he guided her into the cradle of his shoulder and nuzzled the wispy tendrils of hair at her temple, she felt her resolve slipping. Then he trailed butterfly kisses down her cheek that ignited a fire within her before he stopped at the corner of her mouth.

"I think you've bewitched me," he murmured, feathering moist kisses back across her cheek to nibble at the sparkling gem on her earlobe. "You haunt my dreams. I try to put you out of my mind, and then I find myself racking my brain to identify your perfume. What is it?"

The question caught her by surprise and she had to concentrate to answer. Her voice was a bare whisper of sound. "Roses and lilacs. A special blend my grandmother made for my twenty-first birthday."

He murmured in response, raising his hand from where his thumb had been lightly stroking her clenched fist. Michelle was amazed to feel his fingers tremble slightly as he tipped her face upward from the shelter of his shoulder. Slowly, almost reverently, he lowered his head to touch her waiting lips, his gaze holding hers in the dim light from the street.

Michelle hadn't realized how tense she'd been until she relaxed under the teasing persuasion of Alec's mouth against hers. She parted her lips, but he didn't deepen their kiss. Tentatively she allowed her hand to glide over his chest just as she had earlier on the dance floor. Though he stiffened at her touch, his heart was pounding and his skin was damp through the silk of his shirt. She was fascinated by the effect she had on him.

He raised his head abruptly, breaking the contact of their lips; just her fingers reached the bare skin above his collar. She opened her eyes to find him frowning down at her, a sigh escaping his lips. Before she could question his sudden withdrawal, the taxi came to a stop.

Alec practically jumped from the car, shoving a handful of bills at the driver without even looking at the amount. After helping her from the taxi, he grasped her elbow and hustled her into the building.

He continued to act strangely as they waited for the elevator, tapping the seconds off with his foot. She didn't know what had happened. One minute he was the passionate lover and the next, a hyperactive escort. Alec shot forward the minute the elevator doors opened, taking her with him, never saying a word. With his finger he stabbed at the number panel, then leaned heavily against the wall of the elevator, keeping the width of the car between them. Michelle gave him a curious look, but he refused to meet her glance.

This is ridiculous. You're being ridiculous. The words were an endless refrain in Alec's mind. He was running scared from something that had teased his brain since Michelle's second dance partner had whisked her away from their table. He'd been green with jealousy; only his strength of will kept him from starting a brawl and dragging Michelle off to the nearest hotel room to stake his claim. He'd just barely managed to avoid making a total ass of himself.

Now, instead of being an ass he was behaving like a lunatic. For some reason, the apartment seemed like a safe haven. Back in his apartment he would return to normal. He needed a sense of normalcy, a return to the life he'd had just over a week ago, before the strawberry blonde with the Bambi eyes had slept in his bed.

He almost groaned audibly when they stepped into the apartment. Glynn had set the stage for a romantic evening. A single light burned over the bar. The meticulous servant had left a bottle of wine chilling on the coffee table in front of the windows. The only thing missing was burning candles.

Michelle didn't speak. She drew off her shawl and languidly dropped it on a chair as she walked by on her way to the windows. Alec loosened his tie and opened his collar, hoping to relieve the constricted feeling in his throat. The apartment wasn't the safe haven he'd anticipated. Instead he found himself inexorably drawn to the woman standing before the nightscape of the city.

Alec raised his hands to the reddish gold cloud of Michelle's hair. He wasn't surprised that his hands trembled as he drew out the two gem-encrusted combs that secured her silken tresses, which, when freed, cascaded over her shoulders like a molten waterfall. He could almost feel the soft curtain caressing his naked body as it had their first night together. For a moment he allowed himself the luxury of burying his face in the softness, nuzzling the curve of her neck.

After this first hesitant caress, he couldn't contain his need any longer. His hands had barely touched her shoulders, when Michelle turned willingly into his embrace. She entwined her hands behind his neck, pulling his head down until their lips met. Like a man dying of thirst, he drank in her sweetness, his fingers losing themselves in her hair. He surrendered himself to the inevitable. He was going to make love to Michelle again.

With his tongue he explored the delicate line of her lips before delving farther. He couldn't withhold his moan of need as he slid his hands up her rib cage. Picturing her dressed only in her fancy lingerie, he cupped her breast, his thumb stroking the upper swell beneath the thin chiffon covering. She shivered and moved against him, murmuring softly in the back of her throat.

He wouldn't wait any longer. Swiftly he lifted her in his arms and began walking steadily toward his bedroom. Just as he came to the doorway, he gave in to temptation, stopping to kiss her parted lips. A single kiss wasn't enough. He placed her on her feet once more, pressing her tightly to him.

"Hey, is anyone home?"

At first Alec thought he'd imagined the feminine voice. No one else was in the apartment except Glynn, who was in his room.

"Come on, Philip. I don't think anyone's here. Alec must have gone out for the evening and given Glynn the night off."

"Well, it's a good thing you brought your key. I wasn't looking forward to sitting in the hallway until someone came home."

"Yes, dear. You get the bags while I turn on some lights. There should be a switch right—oops."

The conversation between the man and woman finally broke through Alec's passion-clouded brain. Not only were there others in the apartment, their voices sounded familiar, very familiar. He turned at the same moment the overhead light came on. By the doorway stood his sister and her husband.

Before he could say a word, Michelle made a very strange noise. He glanced back at her and froze. She was staring at Jessica with a horrified look on her face. "Oh, my Lord, it's your... ah... wife!"

No one moved once Michelle spoke, her words echoing in the stillness of the room. Then Philip dropped the suitcases he was holding. Michelle's eyes remained on Jessica, though. She was aware of Alec's gaze moving back and forth between his sister and her. As she had so many times in the past, she decided to follow Jessica's lead.

"Darling, aren't you going to introduce us to your companion?" Jessica asked sweetly, taking the opportunity to wink at her friend while her brother released Michelle.

"Uh, Jess, this is Michelle Moens," Alec began hesitantly, still alternating his gaze between the two women. "Michelle, this is Jessica and Philip Benedict."

Michelle nodded and tried to keep her lips from quivering at his stilted speech. He managed to introduce everyone properly without lying outright, yet she doubted if it was his intention to introduce Jessica and Philip as husband and wife. Jessica appeared to feel the same way, judging from her raised eyebrows.

Although Michelle had no idea why her friend was there, she was extremely grateful. In another few minutes she would have been back in Alec's bed without a whimper of protest. She needed Jessica as protection. Yes, she acknowledged, there may have been a few, fleeting minutes of sanity when Alec had behaved so strangely upon their return to the apartment. But the moment he took her in his arms again, she forgot everything else.

"Alec, have we come at a bad time?" Jessica asked, breaking the silence. "There was some news we wanted to share with you, but it can wait."

"I don't want to delay any family business," Michelle announced, suddenly very conscious of her disheveled appearance. Walking toward her room, she paused to pick up her shawl and purse, resisting the urge to straighten her hair. "I'll go on to bed so you can talk to your wife."

"There's that word again," Philip muttered, and received a quelling look from Jessica.

"No, Ms Moens, you can stay. Alec and I have no secrets," Jessica quickly assured her with a triumphant grin. Then she looked at her brother, who was still staring fixedly at Michelle, and ran her eyes pointedly over his loosened tie and unbuttoned shirt. "Do we, Alec?"

"Do we what? Um, I don't think there's any reason for Michelle to leave," he answered vaguely, clearly having no idea what he was saying.

"Yes, let's do be civilized, shall we?" Jessica agreed without any malice as she removed her raincoat and tossed it over the bar. She pushed back the cuffs of her shirt and walked around the back of the bar. "I'll make everyone a nice drink."

Michelle gave a helpless shrug and put down her shawl and purse again with a resigned sigh as Philip followed his wife to the bar. She took a quick look at Alec, who was rooted to the spot where he stood. Now that her initial pleasure over her best friend's arrival had subsided, she felt very uneasy. Jessica was in a suspiciously good mood.

"What's your poison these days, Alec?" his sister asked airily from behind the bar.

"I'll have a club soda, and make Michelle a Canadian Mist and soda."

"Teetotaling? How strange. So am I," declared Jessica as she quickly prepared their drinks. Philip hovered at her side, a frown marring his tanned face. Jessica handed him two glasses and nudged him toward the others. She joined him, then remained standing while everyone else took a seat. "Well, you're probably wondering why we're here."

"The thought had crossed my mind," Alec returned dryly. He studied his sister over the rim of his glass as if she were a repellent insect.

Michelle wanted to crawl into her room and hide. She wasn't sure what was coming, but she knew Jessica too well. Her friend hadn't come all the way from California for an innocent visit. She had a purpose, which was probably to wreak havoc. Her dear former roommate was standing at the center of the room, wringing all the drama out of the moment.

"We have wonderful news. The doctor told me yesterday I'm two months pregnant," Jessica announced, giving everyone a measured look before she continued. "So you see, Alec, you'll have to divorce me now so Philip can marry me. I want the baby to be legitimate."

I'm going to kill her with my bare hands. It will be justifiable homicide. Michelle gripped the arms of her chair to keep herself from jumping up. When she looked at the two men, she realized she would prob-

ably have to stand in line for the privilege of commit-
ting murder. Both had barely managed to keep from
choking on their drinks and were now staring at Jessica. Although on second glance, Philip's expression
was one of suppressed amusement.

"Really, Jess, dear, you could've softened the announcement just a little," Philip admonished when no
one else spoke.

"Yes, dear Jessica, your . . . ah, Philip is right," Alec
agreed, an edge to his voice. Suddenly looking very
tired, he dragged a weary hand through his hair, "I
think we should wait and discuss this further in the
morning. A good night's sleep should improve everyone's outlook—or at least it should improve mine.
Maybe."

"You're probably right, although you've always been
more of a morning person than me," Jessica agreed
readily, apparently not the least bit put out that no one
had congratulated her about the baby. She walked to
the bar and set down her glass. Casually she turned
back to the group—too casually. "What are the sleeping arrangements? I assume there are still only two
bedrooms?"

"Yes, Miss Jess, that's right," Glynn answered from
the doorway to the kitchen.

"Glynn!" Jessica squealed, and ran over to give the
older man a tight hug. "How are you with diapers and
baby formula?"

"I've held up under other disasters, so I suppose I can
handle one of your babies," he answered evenly.
"However, your immediate need seems to be a place to
sleep. Might I suggest that you use the fold-out chair-

bed in Miss Michelle's room and that the two gentlemen take the master bedroom."

"This certainly won't be the first time we've roomed together," Philip said agreeably. He was on his feet quickly, and moved to separate the luggage still piled at the front door.

"Since that's all settled, I'll go to bed." Michelle stood, grabbed her possessions and crossed the room before anyone could say a word. She knew it was past time to have a talk with Jessica about this farce. "Philip, you can bring Jessica's bags in here. I think we should be on a first-name basis since we're rooming together. Good night, everyone."

She didn't bother to look back. Through the open doorway she heard Jessica say, "I think Michelle has the right idea. It's time to hit the sack."

"She'd better be careful, or that's not the only thing that's going to get hit," Philip muttered as he put down his wife's suitcases next to the bed. He grinned at Michelle, then winked.

"Why are you going along with this?" she asked in a whisper.

"You know Jess." With a sheepish smile he rubbed the back of his neck. "Ask Jess how Alec acted when we got engaged."

He kissed Michelle on the cheek and left the room. A few minutes later Jessica entered. Shutting the door, she leaned against it, giggling helplessly. After a few minutes she managed to control her laughter enough to realize Michelle was standing by the bed, her arms crossed over her chest. She wasn't laughing.

"Are you out of your tiny, little brain? 'I'm pregnant and I want my baby to be legitimate'?"

"One of my better moments, wasn't it?" Jessica ignored the other woman's biting tone. She walked to the bed and plopped herself down, kicking off her shoes. Propped up on her elbows, she studied her friend. "Aren't you glad the cavalry is here?"

"I'm not sure, General Custer, but I'm going to change clothes before we start any lengthy discussions." Michelle moved toward the closet, unzipping her dress as she walked. "While I change, you can tell me why Philip is cooperating. It has something to do with your engagement."

"Don't get mad, get even. That's my Philip." Jessica laughed, but then almost choked at the sight of Michelle without her dress. "Gad, I don't think you needed the cavalry, after all. That's practically indecent."

"Merely *Grand-mère*'s sage advice about the psychological advantage of dressing to improve my frame of mind."

"That wouldn't improve Alec's, that's for sure. It would turn his brain to tapioca," Jessica remarked with a whistle. "I think I've mistaken a tigress for a kitten all these years."

"Don't get your hopes up," Michelle called from the bathroom. "I'm still a kitten without claws, in spite of the fancy wrapping, which, incidentally, itches."

"I'm not so sure, little one," Jessica said when Michelle came back into the bedroom. She eyed her friend's braided hair and satinette nightshirt. "Now that's the Hal I know."

"And so does Glynn, by the way. You still didn't tell me about Alec and your engagement," Michelle prompted as she sat cross-legged at the foot of the bed.

"You know Alec and Philip were in college together. That's how I met him, when he came to visit big brother during a business trip." Jessica waited for Michelle's nod. "Big brother wasn't quite sure his friend was good enough for his baby sister when we got engaged. He made Philip's life miserable before he gave his permission."

"His permission? You've got to be kidding."

"Cross my heart. There's no limit to the arrogance of a Lindfors man. They never explain or apologize. They just give orders." Jessica sighed. "Unfortunately—for them—Lindfors women are *very* stubborn."

"I'll just bet they are." Michelle chuckled, remembering the look on Alec's face when Jessica had asked for her "divorce." "We'd better get some sleep, Fred. You've got some serious explaining to do for big brother tomorrow."

"How true. I think the sheets and extra blanket are on the closet shelf." Jessica rolled off the end of the bed in one agile movement. Within a few minutes she had the single bed pulled out of the armchair and had retrieved the bedding from the closet. "That should do it."

"You want to flip for the double bed?" Michelle asked while Jessica riffled through her suitcase.

"No, thanks, it's too firm for me," Jessica replied eyeing the bed in question with distaste before heading for the bathroom with her cosmetic case. "I'll take the nice, soft single one since I'm sleeping for two now."

Michelle started to laugh, but sobered quickly and sat upright to replay their conversation. She'd just assumed her friend was joking about her pregnancy because of the absurd way Jessica had made the announcement. She jumped to her feet, almost run-

ning the few steps to the bathroom door. Jessica was
bent over the sink, brushing her teeth. She turned her
head and raised her eyebrows to question her friend's
precipitous arrival.

Michelle swept a measuring glance over Jessica's
slender pajama-clad figure. If her guess was correct, the
blue-and-white striped cotton trousers and shirt were
Philip's. She put her hands on her hips and demanded,
"Are you actually pregnant?"

At first only the sound of running water answered
her. Jessica rinsed her toothbrush and took a few sips
of water. Very carefully she placed the glass back in its
holder next to her toothbrush. Slowly she turned toward her friend with a big, toothy grin spreading across
her face and flung her arms wide. "Yes!"

"Hallelujah! That's terrific," Michelle squealed. She
grabbed Jessica in an enthusiastic hug. "You nut. No-
body paid any attention with all that divorce drivel."

"After three years of trying, doesn't it make sense to
tell your family in person? Why else do you think I got
Philip on the plane today?"

"What a rat. I'm going to be an auntie of sorts, and
you treat it like a joke." Michelle walked back into the
bedroom and flopped on the bed. "I think you'd better
let Alec know first thing tomorrow morning."

"You are the bossiest woman at times," Jessica complained as she climbed into her own bed. "I have a feeling big brother will have a few other things on his mind
in the morning."

"Better you than me."

"Well, while you're making plans to be a godmom-
mie in seven months, you can also come up with a good

version about what you and Alec were doing when we arrived."

A smug smile and Jessica's twinkling blue eyes were the last things Michelle saw before the lamp between the beds was snapped off. She groaned and rolled onto her side, pulling the sheet over her head to block out her friend's knowing snicker. Memories of Alec were going to keep her awake most of the night without her worrying about Jessica's pointed questions.

Michelle flounced over onto her back, not caring if she disturbed Jessica. After all, Jessica was responsible for getting her into this dilemma. *Well, partially responsible*, she amended with a few minutes of consideration, *but he is her brother*.

She'd never felt so guilty in her entire life. All she could see was Alec's tired and bewildered face as he'd stood in the middle of the living room, trying to absorb Jessica's fairy tale. Whatever anger she'd had toward him was gradually slipping away.

She still thought Alec was stupid for masquerading as a married man. He was purposely missing any opportunities to find a lifetime partner, just as she was by hiding behind her misplaced guilt over Stuart. For three years she'd shied away from any emotional involvement, and now found herself too susceptible to the first handsome man who paid her the least little attention. Or would she have responded so readily to anyone else but Alec?

The thought terrified her. But then she told herself it was only a physical attraction she felt for the man. He was an expert at manipulating women, making love to them. Unfortunately, images of Alec holding and kissing other women made her feel even worse.

I have stunted emotional growth, that's all. Emotional retardation is my problem. I can't be falling in love with Alec. Michelle flung herself onto her stomach and gave a snort of disgust. The evening had started so happily. Dozens of men had vied for her attention, and Alec had been enthralled by her . . . *Oh, damn.*

She wouldn't think about him anymore. Instead of counting sheep, she would rehearse her reasons to Jessica for stopping this joke. Knowing Jessica, the reasons would have to be airtight. She wasn't sure who she wanted to keep from being hurt, Alec or herself. However, tomorrow morning all pretenses would be over. She would simply be the Comtron representative checking the Lindfors computer. Any further relationship with Alec would be strictly business.

ALEC WAS BEGINNING to think that Philip had drowned in the shower, when the water finally shut off. He hadn't had a chance to question his old friend about what had happened in the living room because Philip had gone straight into the bathroom. Until now Alec always thought of himself as a patient man, but the past fifteen minutes had seemed like hours as he'd sat waiting for an explanation for his own, personal Twilight Zone.

Why did I ever say that Jess was my wife? Stupid, stupid, stupid. Of course, having an extremely unpredictable sister only made matters worse, he decided. Jessica just loved to play games. After Michelle had called her his wife, she must have figured out what was going on. Only now he didn't want the protection of a fictitious wife anymore, not with Michelle. Unfortunately his sister had taken the opportunity to loyally, but misguidedly, help him out. He dropped his head forward, digging his fingers into his scalp.

"You know, I may be from California, but I refuse to sleep with a guy in a ruffled shirt," Philip announced from the bathroom doorway. He leaned negligently against the doorjamb, his hands shoved in the pockets of his robe. His expression was tinged with amusement.

"Cute, Benedict," Alec snapped as he brought his head up to glare at his brother-in-law. "Has my dear sister suffered any new head injuries lately, or is it still the same old problem of having been dropped on her head during delivery?"

"It beats me. I'm just along for the ride, though lunacy seems to be running rampant in the family." Philip dropped his shaving kit onto his suitcase. "Why are you suddenly married to my wife, your sister?"

Rather than answer immediately, Alec jumped to his feet and walked to his dresser. He busied himself taking off his dress pumps, his socks and finally his trousers. Dressed only in black briefs, he stalked to the closet, trying to think of a plausible answer. A quick look at his friend, who was vainly trying not to laugh, told him his efforts were futile. With as much dignity as possible he pulled on his robe. He felt less vulnerable at least partially dressed.

"Maybe I should sit down for this," Philip remarked, and seated himself on the end of the bed, an expectant expression on his face. "When you start imitating Glynn, it usually means it's going to be a clinker. Does this have something to do with your ongoing feud with the gossip columnists and your masquerade as a married man?"

"Only I got into this one all by myself," Alec stated, rubbing the back of his neck and giving his friend a chagrined look. "I told Michelle that the picture of Jess in my office was my wife." At his friend's shout of laughter, Alec gave an uncharacteristic shrug of defeat. "It seemed like a good idea at the time just to go along with the old story."

"Until tonight."

"Amazing, isn't it?" Alec asked, still incredulous that one woman could change his entire perspective. He sat down next to his friend, leaning his forearms on his thighs. For a few minutes he stared off into space, reflecting on the changes in his attitude about love and commitment since meeting Michelle.

"Did I ever tell you how I really met your sister?"

Philip's amused question broke through Alec's thoughts. He frowned in concentration, trying to remember. Without turning his head, he answered, "She had dinner with us when you came to town for a convention, wasn't it?"

"Nope, that was the second time. I stopped here at the apartment first that day and was poleaxed by the sight of a very nicely shaped brunette who answered the door in a pink negligee."

"What?"

Philip laughed and pretended to cringe. "Hey, I married her, didn't I? I just told you so you wouldn't think you were the only man in the world this has happened to."

"I wish it was that easy for me," Alec returned in a soft tone, suddenly depressed at the mess his orderly life had become.

"Why couldn't it? Your Michelle seems to be very pleasant as well as being a real knockout."

Alec glared at his friend, knowing his jealous reaction to the admiration in Philip's voice was idiotic. Wearily he rubbed his hand over his mouth and chin. "You go on to bed. I need a bicarb. I'll be back in a minute."

"Try to go easy on Jess tomorrow, will you?" Philip said as he reached the door. "You don't want to upset your future niece or nephew."

"What?" Alec turned to give the other man a measured look. Until that moment, he'd thought all the talk about babies had been part of Jess's little joke.

"You really are going to be an uncle in about seven months," Philip said, a fatuous grin on his face.

"You mean that's the real reason you're here?"

"It's true. After a year of living with a woman attached to a thermometer twenty-four hours a day who picks the darnedest time to poke me and say, 'Now, Philip, now,'" His enormous grin contradicted his disparaging words.

"Well, I'll be damned." Alec closed the distance between them in two strides to grab his brother-in-law in a bear hug.

He left the room minutes later, but the smile on his face at the advent of another Lindfors generation quickly disappeared as he crossed the living room. For some reason Philip's and Jessica's presence, their loving relationship, only intensified his confusion over Michelle. He'd been physically attracted to many women, but never emotionally involved. His feelings were raw, vulnerable, and he wanted to protect himself still from the anguish of exposing them.

Stubbing his toe on a chair leg, Alec ground out an expletive and flipped on the light over the sink to avoid any further mishaps. He didn't need to add bodily injuries to his growing list of troubles. The company was having problems due to one vindictive woman, he was in danger of becoming an emotional wreck over Michelle and his sister's arrival probably guaranteed he'd be wearing a straitjacket soon.

"Where's that blasted bottle?" he grumbled when he couldn't find the familiar glass cylinder in its usual place. His irritation grew as he searched through the adjoining cabinets, then the drawers. Finally he checked Glynn's "junk" drawer as a last resort, only to have it get stuck partway open.

Something was jammed against the top of the drawer frame. Alec swore and muttered under his breath as he jimmied the flat object that was the cause of the problem. After a tug-of-war and a pinched finger he succeeded. "Well, at least one thing is going right."

He pulled the drawer all the way out and froze. Two young women stared up at him from the picture Glynn had said was being repaired. They stared at him from behind clear, unbroken glass and surrounded by a frame in perfect condition.

Almost in slow motion he reached out to pick up the photograph. He was reluctant to take a closer look at Jess's companion, the girl with the long braids and heartbreaking smile. Maybe he was imagining the resemblance, he thought in desperation, and carefully laid the picture on the counter, closer to the light. He saw Michelle's sweet face everywhere; why not in an old photograph, too?

It's not my imagination. It is Michelle. Now he understood his sense of déjà vu the night before. Her single braid reminded him of the picture he'd carried with him for so long. It had been a bright reminder of home, along with Jess's chatty letters about her four friends' college adventures. He lost himself in Jess's letters, which brought the peaceful simplicity of home to a place torn apart by war. He'd been surrounded by dirt and death in a foreign country and the letters and photograph of Jess and one of her roommates had helped preserve his sanity.

The picture of the two smiling faces had been propped up next to his hospital bed when they'd operated time and time again to remove the shell fragments from his legs. It had helped renew his courage during the pain of his physical therapy. Alec had begun to feel that he knew each one of Jess's close friends, personally, that he'd been invited to join their charmed circle.

Now his sister and her college roommate were sharing a room again, probably giggling and snickering over their little masquerade. He swore at length, gripping the countertop to keep from stomping into the guest room and yanking them out of bed. What amazed him was that there were only two of them to torment him, not all four of the faithful friends he'd read about in Jess's letters.

As he recalled, one had been a dancer and another had been an aspiring actress, but Jess had written the most about the shy, younger one they called "Hal," a male nickname for "Henry" or a feminine nickname for "Henrietta." Michelle Henrietta Moens, who'd spent the better part of the past week making a fool of him, making him fall in love with her. *There I've admitted it, now that I know it was all a huge joke*, he thought grimly.

Or was it? Could Michelle have responded so ardently and not felt anything for him? Alec shook his head in denial, the gesture seeming necessary. Her velvet brown eyes had held desire whenever he'd kissed her, and perhaps a small measure of apprehension, almost as if she were frightened by her own emotions. Perhaps some of her shyness remained after fifteen years. He might be deluding himself, but he couldn't believe she was deceiving him. He didn't want to believe it.

The thought almost made him laugh. He'd never anticipated that love would hit him this hard. He was perfectly willing to believe his sister and his old friend Glynn would readily play this humorless joke, but not Michelle. Glynn's guilt was evident; he'd hidden the picture and been responsible for "accidentally" putting Michelle in the master bedroom. Good, old Jess might be pregnant; however, he doubted very seriously that her condition would make her forget her oldest and dearest friend. He just couldn't muster any anger against Michelle. She couldn't be guilty of this hoax.

Carefully he put the picture back in the drawer. He would play along until he discovered exactly who was involved in the charade. Tomorrow morning he'd go to the house in Lake Forest to get some answers. Somewhere in the attic Jessica's letters were moldering, along with hundreds of other useless items his mother refused to part with. Even though he hadn't gone through his gear since he'd returned from Vietnam, he was sure it was safely stored in the attic.

He had to see if his memory of Jess's letters about Michelle's past life was accurate. It was possible he'd spun some fantasies around her innocent face years before.

7

"WELL, LOOK what finally crawled out of the guest room," Jessica announced with irritating good humor when Michelle crossed the living room to the dining area, still in her nightshirt and robe. Her jubilant friend was wolfing down an indecent quantity of food.

"Good morning, Philip. Isn't she supposed to be having morning sickness or something equally unpleasant?" Michelle asked, pointedly ignoring Jessica.

"Ah, Miss Hal, you've joined the other children for breakfast," Glynn said from the kitchen doorway, frowning his disapproval at Jessica. "Fortunately you missed the food fight a few minutes ago."

"I only flicked a piece of toast at Philip," Jessica explained when Michelle raised her brows inquiringly, "just as Glynn came out of the kitchen to freshen our coffee."

Michelle didn't bother answering and gave Glynn, who was hovering, her request for breakfast. She was grateful he solicitously poured her coffee before he returned to the kitchen. While Philip and Jessica affectionately squabbled she used the stimulant to fortify her courage. Glynn had called her by her nickname so she knew Alec wasn't on the premises. She had the perfect opportunity to stop their stupid game. Her mind was firmly set despite her restless night of dreaming about Alec's lovemaking.

"Hal, you tell Philip that the baseball game this afternoon is out of the question," Jessica exclaimed, obviously not sharing her husband's idea of entertainment. "Sitting in the bleachers at Wrigley Field is not romantic. You can't make progress with Alec at the ballpark."

"It doesn't matter, Fred, because I'm going to tell Alec the truth." Michelle confessed all in one breath before she lost her nerve. Jessica had involved her in too many scrapes in the past by the sheer momentum of her enthusiasm. If she could head Jessica off before she got wound up, success might be possible.

However, she didn't anticipate the reaction to her quiet statement. Everyone froze, staring at her as if she'd lost her mind. Philip held his coffee cup in midair, while Jessica sat with her mouth agape. Even Glynn was nonplussed, momentarily paralyzed mid-stride as he carried her English muffins and juice from the kitchen. Michelle wanted to sink down in her chair and disappear under the table. Instead she reached for her coffee with a slightly unsteady hand, trying to act as if everything were very normal.

"No, you can't do it."

Michelle almost choked on the hot coffee she was sipping at the vehement statement that broke the tableau. She stared at Philip, incredulous that the usually quiet, good-natured man was the one opposing her. Jessica's cajoling or Glynn's imperious stare she'd expected, but she never thought that Philip would even take sides in the discussion.

"What?" she said, deciding she must have imagined the words. Carefully she put her cup on its saucer, allowing Glynn room to place her breakfast in front of her.

"I said, 'You can't do it.' You've done something no one else has managed to do in years," Philip answered, his expression earnest. He paused and gave Michelle an encouraging smile. "You've turned him back into a human being."

"Here, here," Glynn murmured, picking up Philip's and Jessica's empty plates.

"Of course he's a human being," she shot back in astonishment, and winced at her petulant tone. She couldn't believe she'd already lost control without Jessica having said a word. Helplessly she watched Jessica order Glynn to forget the dishes and join them at the table. The three of them were going to gang up on her, and for some bizarre reason she was defending Alec.

"Yes, he is, after a week of your charming company, Miss Hal," Glynn agreed as he took a seat next to Philip. "Until you arrived I was tempted to check his pulse to see if he was real or a robot."

"For heaven's sake, Glynn made a joke," Jessica said admiringly, a look of surprise on her face. "He isn't really kidding, though, Hal. Alec's been driving himself since he had to take over the business when Dad died. All he does is work continually and socialize because it's expected of him."

"Because he's expected to socialize? I wasn't born under a cabbage leaf," Michelle responded with a sharp laugh. She quashed a little voice inside her that asked, *why not?* "A man doesn't get his picture in the paper with every unattached woman in Chicago because he's expected to do it."

"Come on, Michelle, you know the corporate world better than any of us," Philip put in when his wife gave a frustrated groan. "A company president has certain obligations in any community. In a city the size of Chicago they multiply, and he's expected to have a companion if he's single."

"So he takes out a variety of attractive women, they're photogenic and keep getting in the newspapers," Jessica broke in eagerly, sitting forward and leaning her elbows on the table. "Soon it becomes newsworthy to see and be seen with the eligible Mr. Lindfors. However, Alec doesn't give a damn about anything but his business."

"Wait just a minute, lady. What happened to that jerk who was pretending to be married and should be taught a lesson?" Michelle demanded suspiciously, since she'd been suckered yet again into another of her best friend's schemes.

"Hey, I'm not saying he wasn't a jerk to do that, but that doesn't mean he's the lech of the century," his sister returned with a wide-eyed look of surprise, seemingly amazed that anyone would doubt her.

"Bull." Michelle uttered the word clearly. She smiled triumphantly at the three faces watching her every move. These people weren't going to wear her down, no matter what the bait. No matter how much she wanted them to be right.

"Nice mouth."

"Jess, don't get ugly. I don't think you want to choose between your brother and your best friend." Philip's gentle tone helped lessen the tense atmosphere.

"And I'm not going to clean it up if anyone starts throwing food again," Glynn added for good measure, causing everyone to break up at his dignified threat.

"Okay, I overreacted a little when you called," Jessica admitted reluctantly when their laughter subsided. She gave a halfhearted, apologetic shrug. "You gave me a golden opportunity to help both you and Alec. You needed to snap out of the blue funk you've been in since you dumped that twerp Stuart, and Alec needed to rediscover the human race."

"Should I salivate when you ring a bell?" Michelle couldn't resist the gibe, torn between irritation and affection. While part of her was angry that she'd been manipulated, another part was pleased her friend cared enough to bother. Unfortunately she was left in an untenable position. Jessica never intended for her to break Alec's heart, and Michelle was beginning to doubt that was her own intention, either.

She looked at the three faces watching her anxiously from across the table while her mind replayed a montage of Alec's handsome face: the way he looked when he kissed her; his smile with that endearing single dimple; his tired, confused look just last night. Could she continue their game now that she knew there was a new purpose?

"Miss Hal, would you please reconsider? Alec needs to have someone to care about." Glynn's face wasn't devoid of expression. He no longer masked his concern. His gray eyes searched her face for a glimmer of a reaction. "I've known him since the war. He started to grow up in Vietnam, and he went back to college to please his father. Then his father died two months before graduation."

"Daddy's heart attack shocked all of us, but Alec felt he'd never proved himself—redeemed himself, actually—for flunking out of school and being drafted," Jessica continued, her expression as concerned as Glynn's. "You've never failed at an academic goal. Alec never doubted himself in anything, then he found he couldn't charm his way out of bad grades or a draft notice."

"He let down his dad badly just that once, but he's still trying to make up for it by driving himself constantly," Philip continued for his wife, who blinked away her tears with a self-conscious sniffle. "At college we could divert him occasionally. He graduated in two and a half years. When his dad died suddenly, he threw himself into the business and hasn't come up for air since. I don't think he's even taken a vacation in ten years."

"If you don't say something soon, I'm going to drag out the violins and oboes," Jessica prompted when Michelle still hadn't responded. "How about a full performance of *Swan Lake*?"

Michelle smiled and put her hands up in surrender. She knew they wouldn't stop until she gave in. Soon they'd be dredging up his first day of kindergarten. Of course, she could counter with tales of his passionate and considerate lovemaking. Somehow the thought was more disturbing than comforting.

"Next you'll drag out the comfy chair," she quipped, naming an absurd form of torture from Monty Python, but it seemed to relieve her three friends. "I'll wait until the end of the week or as soon as I finish with the computer, whichever comes first."

"You won't regret this, I promise."

Although Jessica was sincere, Michelle was sure she would indeed regret this, very much. Alec was dangerous to her peace of mind, and a strictly business relationship would be her salvation. She didn't know what she could do to help a suave, sophisticated man with Alec's looks. However, she knew she was through playing tricks; from this point on she'd be herself. No more dressing up or playing the vamp.

"Are you sure I'm the right woman to do this?"

"Yes," replied three voices in unison, and Jessica, Philip and Glynn stood up quickly, as though they thought she might change her mind if they remained seated at the table.

"Come on, roomie, we need to get our baseball togs on, since it looks like we'll be going to visit the Cubbies when big brother gets back," Jessica pronounced cheerfully, flinging an arm around Michelle's shoulders. "Don't look so grim. Wait until you hear what Olivia and I cooked up for Patrice. You may be the only person she's speaking to by the end of next week."

ALEC AUTOMATICALLY steered his silvery-gray Rolls Corniche up the slight incline of his driveway. He cut the engine and sat still, reluctant to enter the house. After an unsettling night picturing Michelle laughing at him, he was depressed. He wasn't so sure anymore that she was a pawn. Slowly he got out of the car, not caring that the sun was shining in a cloudless blue sky. The usually welcoming facade of the neo-Tudor house that sat nestled among the trees now seemed cold and forbidding.

The smell of furniture polish as he mounted the three flights of stairs told him Mrs. Scott had been there the day before to clean. He paused before the locked door that closed off the third floor. For a moment he fingered his keys and considered leaving without looking for the letters. Then he squared his shoulders and unlocked the door to the old servants' quarters, now a haven for junk. He needed to know for certain if he'd been a total fool to fall in love with Michelle.

He smiled humorlessly as he moved down the short hallway. His mother's idea of organization was assigning each of the four rooms to specific people's possessions. The second room on the right was for Jessica and him.

He waded through the debris to the window, thankful he'd worn old jeans and a chambray shirt. Shapeless forms became long-forgotten possessions once he raised the blinds. Jess's Tiny Tears doll leaned drunkenly against his half-deflated football. Two sets of mortarboards and tassels were stacked alongside high school yearbooks in a baby buggy. Then his eye was caught by the squared end of a dull khaki box peeking from beneath Jessica's pompoms.

Quickly he dragged the foot locker out and pulled it under the window. Inside everything was neatly placed. The oilskin packet was right on top. His heartbeat accelerated slightly when he actually held the package of letters in his hand. Hastily he closed the trunk and sat on the lid, then, leaning back against the windowsill, he tore the string binding away.

The blue air-mail letters were in separate bundles for each year. The old rubber band fell apart in his hand when he pulled it from around the stack marked with the year Jess had started college. Almost three-fourths of the way through the pile he found where she'd first mentioned her roommates.

By the time he came to the end of the second letter he realized he was grinning like an idiot. Jess had been very maternal toward her shy, sixteen-year-old friend from the minute they'd met. She described Michelle as a frightened little rabbit with huge brown eyes, a girl totally without self-confidence. The mention of her age reminded Alec of Michelle's first conversation with Lew about skipping grades in school. His misplaced jealousy then had been the first warning he was interested in her as more than a bed partner.

Jess faithfully reported each incident that had gradually brought Michelle out of her reclusive shell. Everything had come to a head one night when Michelle confessed to what she thought was her horrible secret. Until she was fourteen, she had been fat and under five-foot tall. Everyone she knew called her, affectionately, "Pudge." Even though she'd grown five inches and lost all her baby fat, "Pudge" was still part of her self-image wherever she went, especially meeting new people. Once the problem was out in the open, his exuberant sister had taken charge.

He thought about how diverting—and almost unreal—Jessica and Michelle's college adventures had seemed to him as a hardened serviceman and therefore a man of the world. Now that he was personally involved, he dreaded reading about each of Michelle's successes with men. A rational part of his mind told him he was crazy to be upset, but he still felt as if someone were strangling his heart when Jess described the first time Michelle imagined she was in love.

Suddenly he didn't want to read any more. After all, he reasoned with a look at his watch, he'd found out what he wanted to know and it was time to get back to the apartment. He slipped the letters into their protective pouch and stood up to slap the dust from his jeans. Immediately he was full of nervous energy. He ran down all three flights of stairs, whistling happily and tossing the packet of letters up in the air. On the ground floor he made a brief stop in the study to retrieve a precious item from the safe before walking briskly to his car.

Even the weekend drivers on Lakeshore Drive didn't bother him while he made his way back to the city. His strawberry-blond swan had been a chubby, superintelligent duckling. He began humming a tune, punctuating the refrain by slapping the steering wheel.

If he knew anything about his loony sister, it was that she felt compelled to interfere when she felt it necessary. Her letters only confirmed that she was used to pushing Michelle for her own good. He'd fallen right into the trap along with Michelle. However, he determined judiciously, if Jessica thought he was what was good for her friend, he would be the last person to disagree. Jessica had shown amazing perception for a change, even if her methods were bizarre.

Later he'd find out all the details that had started the game. He'd play his part enthusiastically with the basic facts he knew. When it suited him, he'd take control. With some skillful maneuvering, Jessica would be the one with egg on her face, instead of him. He'd make sure she wouldn't be so eager to start her next scheme once he won Michelle over.

For the next few miles Alec amused himself with various fantasies: Jessica, Philip and Glynn all taking turns in numerous devices in a well-appointed torture chamber; while they were being taken care of so satisfactorily, he'd spend his days and nights with Michelle making love. He came abruptly out of his dream when he realized he was passing the Water Tower and would have to double back for the street to his apartment.

"DIDN'T I TELL YOU the bleachers were the most terrific place to sit?" Philip shouted in an effort to be heard over the catcalls and boos of the surrounding spectators.

I'm going to make his death slow and very painful. A scorching look accompanied Alec's thought as yet another fan returning from the concession stand tripped over him. His high expectations when he'd returned to the apartment had been immediately deflated the second he learned about plans for the afternoon. Besides the fact that he couldn't spend any time alone with Michelle, he hated baseball, noisy crowds and sitting in the hot sun for no good reason. Except for the fact that Michelle's body was continually pushed up against him during the tedious no-hitter, the entire excursion was a disaster.

"Hey, babe, I'll be glad to pollinate your flower anytime," a surly, guttural voice shouted from one row below.

Alec glared at the squat, beer-bellied idiot leering at Michelle. Or, more accurately, at her well-filled-out T-shirt that announced Pollination in Progress above a huge white daisy with a cartoon bee on its yellow center. He placed a proprietary arm around Michelle's hunched shoulders. She gratefully moved closer, crossing her arms over her chest.

"Did you want something, mister?" At Alec's question the heckler turned hastily back to his loutish friends, signaling he'd caught the dangerous undertone in the query. The man couldn't know his supposedly original offer had been posed at least a half-dozen times since Michelle had removed her Windbreaker in the second inning.

Although Alec loathed the attention the bright green shirt attracted, he appreciated the opportunity it gave him to touch Michelle. He knew she wasn't comfortable in the garment, and for the life of him, he couldn't figure out why she was wearing it. Every suggestive comment aimed at the thin cloth hugging her full breasts like a second skin had her pressing against his side. He took full advantage despite the fact that she looked about seventeen with her hair pulled back into a ponytail that sung all the way down her back and the sprinkling of freckles on her nose that were no longer camouflaged by makeup.

When Michelle leaned away from him to talk to Jessica, he relaxed for a few minutes, wondering how much he could withstand before he grabbed her and kissed her unconscious in front of hundreds of spectators. He heard her ask Jess for directions to the rest room. Before his sister could answer, he decided to take control, giving Michelle's ponytail a playful tweak to get her attention.

"I'll walk down with you."

Michelle nodded and smiled hesitantly in gratitude, knowing—as he did—that Jessica would point her in the right direction and make her fend for herself. Michelle chose him as the lesser of two evils.

He felt a slight twinge of guilt. His offer had been somewhat gallant, but he'd also wanted to snatch a few minutes alone with her, something he hadn't accomplished since Jessica's arrival.

He stood and allowed her to pass in front of him, seeing the back of her T-shirt for the first time. Below the latticed cutout, the bee was now lying on its back, smoking a cigarette with a very satisfied smile on its little insect face. If he'd had a coat or a blanket, anything within reach, he would have thrown it over her. The thought of the bee's satisfaction only intensified the ache inside him. That ache bordered on agony as he watched the sway of her hips in her dark green trail shorts while he followed her single file down the concrete steps.

Once they were on ground level, he captured her hand and they searched for the rest rooms along the shadowy tunnel that circled the stadium. Before he could stop himself he blurted out the thought uppermost in his mind. "Where did you get that T-shirt?"

She looked up at him half-apologetically, and he thought he saw her blush in the dim light. "Philip and Jessica gave it to me. I didn't want to hurt their feelings by not wearing it."

"I like it. I just wish other people didn't like it so much."

"Between you and me, I'm burying it in my closet when I get home," she responded with a mischievous smile. She caught sight of the rest room just then and said nothing further. Reluctantly Alec let go of her hand. Her words had reminded him that she would be going home to Atlanta once his computer problems were solved. On Monday she would no doubt be asking pressing questions about the malfunctions, which wouldn't advance his love life.

He had to have some time alone with her in more intimate surroundings than a seventy-odd-year-old stadium. Jessica and Philip didn't know it yet, but they were going out to dinner and a play, even if Alec had to pay them to do it. At least Glynn had the weekend off and was in Milwaukee until Sunday night.

He smiled as he spotted Michelle's approaching figure, hoping he and her friend the bee would have a great deal in common by the end of the evening.

"I CERTAINLY HOPE you got all of big brother's fingerprints washed off," Jessica commented in a teasing tone as Michelle came out of the bathroom from her shower.

"What are you talking about?" Michelle asked, pulling off her shower cap and shaking out her hair. She turned her back on her friend. Bending at the waist, she flipped her hair over her head and began brushing. After the count of fifty, she straightened, tossing her hair back in a golden cascade.

"Well, I certainly didn't see you objecting to Alec playing the big, brave male when your T-shirt caused a few heads to turn. In fact, you seemed to be enjoying your damsel-in-distress role. I think you've been in the South just a tad too long."

"*My* T-shirt? You traitor. You made me wear it," Michelle exclaimed indignantly, flopping down next to her friend on the bed. She wouldn't admit she'd enjoyed Alec's solicitousness. "I'm planning to burn that rag, even if you did buy it especially for me at the garden show. Landscapers must be slightly deviant."

"Yeah, and if you'd worn an ordinary, bland T-shirt or one of your usual tent blouses, what would Alec have done with his hands all afternoon? He hates baseball." Jessica's smile grew even wider as she headed for the bathroom. "It had some rather interesting results. Philip and I have been told—in no uncertain terms—that we're going out for the evening—Alec's footing the bill. So don't knock that T-shirt."

Michelle stuck out her tongue at the closing bathroom door in response to her friend's smug grin. Then she considered what had taken place during that afternoon. Alec had seemed different today. Or perhaps he was the same, and she was responding differently. She didn't have to worry about vamping him anymore, and could simply be his sister's old friend—even if he didn't know that's what she was. Fluffing her pillows and leaning back against the headboard, she wondered how her new attitude would survive the evening.

He wanted to be alone with her, literally kicking his sister and brother-in-law out the door. If he turned on his potent charm again, she was a goner. All he had to do was kiss her and she was Jell-O. Somehow she had to keep out of his reach, keep him at arm's length.

She chuckled sleepily and yawned. Too much fresh air was making her brain go soft. Closing her eyes for just a minute while she waited for Jessica to come out of the bathroom, she wondered if there was a subtle way to ask her friend for advice. Quickly she dismissed the idea as ridiculous. Jessica would willingly throw her into Alec's arms without batting an eye.

Michelle never heard Jessica come back into the bedroom. She continued to sleep peacefully all the while the other woman dressed to go out for the evening. When Jessica tiptoed out of the room, she murmured contentedly in her sleep and rolled over onto her side.

ALEC WHISTLED HAPPILY, enjoying himself while he gathered everything for his intimate dinner with Michelle. Jessica and Philip had been gone for over an hour. *Cats* was a nice, long play, and with dinner, they'd be gone until the wee hours of the morning.

He danced a little jig, balancing two plates filled with lobster salad and fresh fruit. The two plates safely in the refrigerator, he danced over to place the cheese croissants in the warmer. Everything was ready. A pleasant Chardonnay sat chilling in a bucket on the nest table between two pewter candlesticks whose candles were ready to be lit. All that was needed was the lady, who was mysteriously absent.

The door to the guest room was half-open. He hesitated for a few minutes, wondering if he was worrying too much. Women took longer than men to get dressed, and Michelle had to share the bathroom with his sloppy sister. Still rationalizing, he took a few cautious steps toward the guest room.

He knocked softly, listening for a response. No one answered; there wasn't even a sound of movement. Frowning, he slowly pushed open the door. Michelle was curled on her side, sound asleep. He clenched and unclenched his hands to relieve the sudden rush of desire he felt.

Although her face was innocent in sleep, the rest of her body was all exciting woman. Her robe gaped in a vee all the way to the loosely tied sash at her waist, revealing the tempting swell of her breasts and the smooth skin of her abdomen. The satiny material was pulled taut over the curve of her hip. One leg was bent at the knee, bared all the way to her thigh.

Something was wrong, he realized suddenly. Michelle's usually creamy white skin looked discolored from her knee up to mid-thigh in the shaft of light from the bathroom. Alec covered the distance to the bedside lamp in two strides and switched it on. Just as he'd suspected; it wasn't a trick of the light; Michelle was sunburned. She'd worn shorts to the ball game because of the unseasonably hot weather, and her legs were bright pink. As were her nose and cheeks and arms. He quickly forgot the seductive evening he'd planned in his concern for her tender skin. Gently he placed a hand on her shoulder, softly calling her name.

"Jessica, let me sleep," she whimpered thickly without opening her eyes. When her plea didn't stop the hand shaking her shoulder, she tried to brush it away. "Don't do that."

"Sweetheart, come on. Wake up."

Michelle's eyes flew open. Alec, not Jessica, was kneeling on the bed beside her. For a few befuddled seconds she wondered what he was doing in their dorm room, then reality reasserted itself. He wasn't part of her dream, she realized; she'd fallen asleep while Jessica was in the shower.

"What time is it?" she asked. Her mind functioning again, she was conscious of her lack of clothing. Only her flimsy satin robe covered her naked body. Instinctively she closed the lapels of her robe.

"Just a little after eight," Alec answered, and let go of her shoulder. He leaned to the side, propping himself up on his elbow, seemingly enthralled by her face.

Michelle swallowed nervously under his avid stare. She had no makeup on and she presumed she looked rumpled. No doubt she'd have pillow wrinkles on her cheek if she sat up. Yet Alec's eyes held admiration, and something else.

"Is dinner ready?" She tried not to wince at the inane question.

He took a deep breath that drew her gaze to the golden hairs peeking out the open vee of his sport shirt. His voice was husky and soft in the still room. "Dinner can wait a little. You're going to need some TLC first."

Her breath caught in her throat and her heart pounded in anticipation. She didn't understand what he meant, but it sounded exciting. In fascination she watched his free hand move toward her leg, where he drew a lazy figure eight with his index finger. Suddenly it registered that the skin he was stroking was shocking pink. "Sunburn?" she squeaked in disbelief. Alec wasn't trying to seduce her; he was showing her the sunburn that had come out while she was asleep. She groaned aloud at her own stupidity.

"It's all right, honey," he reassured her, misinterpreting her distress. "We just need to get some cream on it."

His soothing words made her want to cry. He sounded as though he were reasoning with a child. She wanted to tell him she was a grown woman with a woman's needs, not a child to be placated. She moved restlessly against the mattress, trying to deny her disappointment.

"Sweetheart, much as I'm enjoying the view, I think we'd better get you into a more reliable covering."

She hastily looked down. Although she held her robe closed, lying on her side had created a deep cleavage that was highly visible above her clenched hand. Her lower body was still safely covered—almost. Her robe was trapped between her legs, preserving her modesty, but the leg Alec touched was bare up to her hip.

Alec was amazed at his control as her embarrassed flush blended with her already-pink skin. She was so incredibly beautiful and vulnerable. Her deep brown eyes were still drowsy. The pouting bow of her mouth just begged to be kissed. He hadn't resisted the one small chance to touch her, but the trust in her eyes and the hot pink of her skin kept his desire in check.

"We need to see where you're burned," he said, clearing his throat and trying to sound clinical. "I'll close my eyes while you get up."

He forced himself to keep his promise as the mattress shifted under her weight. Her movements seemed interminably slow, even though he knew she was probably stiff from her nap and the sunburn. When he heard her moan, he couldn't be patient any longer, and he opened his eyes.

She knew the minute he turned to look at her. He caught her holding up the bottom of her robe to examine her legs. Aside from her face, only her lower thighs were really burned, along with her arms and a small portion of her back where the T-shirt was cut out.

"Are you all right?"

His harsh demand made her quickly drop the garment back in place. She was blushing again, and he probably thought she was more sunburned than she actually was.

"Go into the bathroom and wrap yourself in one of those oversize towels," Alec ordered briskly, and sprang off the bed. "I'll see what Glynn has in the first-aid kit."

"I—I have some aloe a friend in Florida gave me. It's on the dresser," she said meekly, not really sure what he intended to do once he had the lotion. Part of her wanted to find out, and the other wanted to lock herself in the bathroom.

"Fine, now get in there and change."

Purposely she didn't think; she simply reacted. She avoided looking in the bathroom mirror while she stripped off her robe and wrapped herself in the royal-blue towel. It went around her twice. Secured high over her breasts, the brushed terry cloth fell almost to her knees.

"This is absolutely insane," she muttered, reaching with an unsteady hand for the doorknob. She knew it wasn't insanity. It was love; crazy, inexplicable love.

She'd finally admitted it when she opened her eyes to find Alec's concerned face so close to her own. Somehow he'd stolen her heart. She'd been masking her deeper feelings behind her misplaced anger, labeling them physical attraction. By burying her true feelings, she was subconsciously avoiding being hurt again. Only now she knew that what she'd experienced before was merely infatuation and a need to be part of a relationship.

With Alec she was in love with the man. Behind his polished exterior was someone as vulnerable as her. Something in him had touched her even before Jessica and Philip had pleaded his case, which was why she'd ended up in the unlikely position of defending him. Instinctively she knew that beneath his cynical facade he was seeking love and warmth from another human being.

Swiftly Michelle turned back to the mirror that had intimidated her a few minutes earlier. She carefully arranged her towel, allowing an enticing amount of creamy skin to show. Deliberately she tucked the toweling into her cleavage. She combed her hair down over her right shoulder, thickened her lashes with mascara and placed discreet dabs of perfume at her wrists, elbows and behind her ears.

Satisfied with her appearance, she decided she could be the best-looking lobster in town. *I hope Alec likes seafood,*, she thought.

Her need to give had somehow overshadowed her old self-doubt and insecurity, and she trusted Alec to appreciate the gift of her unspoken love. Her earlier need to protect herself from his magnetism was gone; in its place was a new serenity she'd never experienced. Tonight she was going to forget about Comtron, Lindfors House and Magda Josefsen and concentrate on Alec, her lover. Monday morning would be soon enough to let the rest of the world return with its problems.

She wanted a respite so she could experience every facet of her newly discovered love. She wasn't going to seduce Alec—or allow herself to be seduced by him— for the sake of some cockamamy scheme. Tonight she was going to make love, fully and completely, to the man who needed her.

She walked confidently to the door and grasped the doorknob firmly. For a second she paused to murmur the words that were the source of her courage. "I love you, Alec."

8

ALEC FELT as if he'd been pacing for hours. He began to worry that she would hide herself in the bathroom all night. His impatience got the better of his judgment, and he gave the door a hard slap. Less than two minutes elapsed before it opened, but he held his breath until she stood before him. And when she did, he was stunned by the alluring woman he beheld.

Physical desire shot through him. Only the angry pink coloring of her arms and legs kept him from folding her into his embrace and buying his face in the inviting swell of her breasts. He'd never wanted a woman so much in his life.

Without realizing what he was doing, he reached out to touch the silky fall of her red-gold hair. She gave him a sweet smile of encouragement. "You have incredible hair, like fiery honey," he whispered, barely hearing his own words.

Boldly he gathered a handful of her soft tresses, then pulled back when his fingers grazed the thrusting curve of her breast. He coughed to cover the awkward moment. "Why don't you go sit on the bed, and we'll take care of that sunburn."

This may be harder than I thought, Michelle mused. She followed his gruff directions, smiling to herself when she walked toward the bed. Her face was totally composed when she sat down and pulled the towel up slightly from her knees.

"I think we should do my legs first. Then I can lie down while you do my arms and back."

Alec looked at her as if she'd grown two heads. Then he shook himself and relaxed. He gave her a slightly dazed smile as he walked back to the bed with the plastic bottle of lotion in his hand.

"I'm not holding up dinner, am I?" she asked quickly when he sat down beside her. She wished her voice wouldn't quiver so much. It was caused by excitement, but she was afraid Alec would think she was nervous or even gauche.

"No, we're having a cold supper that's ready whenever we are," he assured her, his head bent as he squeezed lotion into his hand. "I hope this doesn't feel too cold."

Michelle just shook her head when he glanced up. She knew that if she dared open her mouth the only thing that would come out was a nervous giggle. He looked so serious, almost as if he were trying to solve a complex puzzle. Soon, however, the motion of his large hand smoothing the cool liquid over her legs made her amusement fade. In its place was a tingling sensation that had nothing to do with her sunburn.

"Okay, let's take care of your back and arms."

To her sensitive ears, Alec's voice sounded forced— at least she hoped it did. She barely contained a grin of anticipation as she scooted back on the bed and rolled over onto her stomach, carefully tucking her hair beneath her. Every nerve in her body seemed to be right on the surface of her skin. Any second he would touch her again.

I've got to get this over with as soon as possible, Alec told himself. At least her back and arms were safer than her legs, he decided with a sense of relief. Although he was still very conscious of her nudity under the large towel, he wasn't in danger of slipping beyond what was safe.

When he was applying the lotion to her legs, all he thought about was how close his fingers were to the most intimate part of her body. He practically said a prayer of thanksgiving when she rolled onto her stomach. He focused all his attention on his hands as he glided them over her glorious skin in circular movements.

He worked as quickly as possible, barely waiting for the lotion to be absorbed into her skin. His hand was beginning to tingle and burn, almost as if her sunburn were being transferred to him.

"All done," he announced proudly, silently letting out his pent-up breath. "How does that feel?"

"Absolutely terrific. You have wonderful hands," she answered, not bothering to hide her breathlessness. She rolled onto her side, striking what she hoped was an alluring pose, and smiled. "My friend swears by aloe. It takes away the sting imm—"

She broke off in amazement when Alec gave her a curt nod, looked somewhere to the right of her shoulder and suddenly got up. He stomped over to the dresser and put the lotion back with a decided thump. Michelle knew she had to think fast. *This seduction was hard work.* She scrambled to her feet with more haste than grace. With a skipping gait she was behind Alec before he could turn around.

"You get dressed while I get dinner—" Alec swallowed his words in a surprised gulp when he turned and discovered Michelle right next to him. He stared at her as if she were a phantom who'd suddenly materialized out of thin air. "Um, I'll get dinner set up."

"I just wanted to thank you for helping with my sunburn," she said, persevering in spite of the fact that her insides were the substance of marshmallow. While Alec was in shock—and before she lost her nerve—she reached up to tangle her fingers in the thick hair at his temples. By standing on tiptoe she didn't have far to tilt his mouth downward to meet her lips.

He stiffened the moment their lips met. He was going to be noble to the bitter end, which didn't surprise her. She'd known that when he'd applied the lotion to her sunburn so tentatively. She parted her lips against his and felt a slight quiver of response that emboldened her to trace his lower lip with the tip of her tongue.

He couldn't withstand her sweet kiss or the desire that raged out of control within him. For one brief moment he tried to retain some sanity for both of them. "Sweetheart, we can't do this tonight."

She didn't react as he'd anticipated. Her lips never left his when she replied. "Why not? I want you, and you want me, I hope."

He wasn't a man who argued with pure logic. After all, he reasoned, this was exactly what he'd planned to do before he'd discovered her sunburn. Apparently aloe had the healing powers everyone ascribed to it. Both of them were adults, and if she wasn't bothered by her sunburn, then it wouldn't bother him, either. He couldn't continue to argue with himself while she was busy unbuttoning his shirt, anyway.

"Are you seducing me?" he whispered. He managed to break away from the intoxicating touch of her lips. Although he was ready to surrender to the inevitable, he wanted to see her eyes.

"Yes, I am," she whispered back, meeting his searching gaze. She smiled hesitantly, asking for his approval. "How am I doing?"

"Just fine, sweetheart." He chuckled as she waggled her eyebrows suggestively. "Would you mind if I helped a little?"

She could feel her smile break into a full-fledged grin. Confidently she slid her hands up the soft mat of golden hair on his chest. His hands clamped at her hips, he pulled her tightly into the cradle of his thighs. With a rocking motion, he pressed his hardened desire against her softness, imitating the rubbing of her hands as they splayed over his chest. She wound her arms around his neck, pulling his mouth to hers once more.

The moment their lips met, Alec swept her up into his arms. With quick strides he carried her to the bed and placed her on the forest-green bedspread. She was reluctant to loosen her hold around his neck when he started to straighten, afraid he would change his mind.

"Relax, honey, I'm just a little overdressed at the moment," he reassured her, and gently pulled her hands from around his neck. He gave her a wicked grin as he stripped off his shirt. "We were better off the first night we met."

She grinned at him. "I promise not to fall out of bed this time."

Then all amusement died when he stretched out next to her, clad only in low-slung maroon briefs. He trailed his index finger over the creamy expanse of her breasts above the edge of her towel. For breathless moments he kept her in suspense, until his fingers dipped into her cleavage, under the knot that secured the towel.

For the first time Michelle's self-assurance cracked slightly at the thought of Alec seeing her naked in the full light. She'd finally gotten him to overlook her sunburn, but what did she do about the traces of stretch marks and her flabby thighs.

"I've dreamed about this every night since I first found your exquisite body in my bed," he murmured against her skin, his lips following the trail of his finger. His hand started untangling the toweling that was hiding her breasts.

She closed her eyes, unable to watch the look of desire fade from his eyes when he saw her body. She gasped in surprise when the warm moisture of his mouth trailed over her breast and suckled the hardened peak.

"Alec, would you turn off the light?"

He raised his head to look directly into her distressed face. She couldn't read his expression, though he seemed guarded suddenly. His eyes were hidden by half-closed eyelids as he considered her request.

"I want to see you this time, sweetheart, all of you."

His husky request made her heart stop momentarily. Alec still thought they'd made love the night he passed out. She couldn't tell the truth, not now. He wouldn't understand, and she wanted tonight.

She squelched the voices of doubt. She loved Alec and wanted this memory of their time together. He should have everything she had to give. Leaving on the light was a small price to pay.

"Okay." She didn't know what else to say.

He smiled tenderly and ran his finger down her nose, lingering over her mouth, then over her chin and the soft skin of her throat. Finally his teasing touch came to rest in the shadowy valley between her breasts. "How do I get you out of this cocoon? I should've told you to use a hand towel."

His disgruntled tone made her laugh. He gave her a mock look of disapproval, then got to his knees, flashing a devilish smile that sent sparks of excitement through her entire body.

"Cleopatra came to Caesar in a rug, so why should a towel defeat me? There's a very simple solution." Tugging at the end of the towel, he grinned widely. "This won't take a minute."

No sooner had he finished speaking than he grabbed the end of the towel and pulled. Michelle was taken completely by surprise. Suddenly she found herself flipped onto her stomach, then her back. Alec was wrong, she decided, trying to catch her breath; it took less than a minute to roll her out of the towel.

He knew he'd never seen anything as beautiful as the laughing, breathless woman lying in front of him. Her brown eyes sparkled with amusement and lambent desire. The reddish gold curtain of her hair draped her curves from shoulder to thigh. He'd guessed that her earlier hesitation had been due to her memories of childhood. But the lady had no need to doubt her desirability.

"Michelle, you are absolutely gorgeous," he whispered almost reverently, lying down beside her to take her in his arms. He slanted his mouth over her inviting red lips, drinking in her sweetness as if he were parched for her taste.

She felt as if she were being buffeted by a whirlwind, spinning out of control. All her senses were centered on Alec—the feel of his tanned skin, the scent of his aftershave and the musky smell that was uniquely his. His hands were touching and caressing her everywhere. She was pure sensation.

"Alec, it's too good . . . Oh, yes, there. Don't ever stop."

"So beautiful and soft. Yes, sweetheart, touch me there."

Michelle thought she would explode with need. She ached for him to take her. For a moment he left her, reaching over the side of the bed for his jeans while he dragged off his briefs. Her disappointment lasted only a second before she realized he was protecting her. Then he was at her side again, taking them quickly back into the maelstrom of passion.

Just when she thought she had experienced all the pleasure she could stand, he entered her. Her whole being was filled with him. She called out his name as the rhythm of their bodies spun them faster and faster toward fulfillment. He stroked into the heated core of her need in powerful, controlled movements. She tried to accelerate his thrusts, twisting and turning under him. She grasped his lean hips, but didn't have the strength to quicken his pace.

"Be patient, love. Soon, very soon."

His hoarse whisper soothed and excited her. She knew he was taking them closer and closer toward the eye of the hurricane. She moved with him, stroking his hips and taut buttocks with trembling fingers. Her breath caught in her throat when his head lowered once more to her breasts. His lips alternated between her aching pleasure points, taking her another step closer to the peak of her desire.

Suddenly she was there, poised on the brink of ecstasy, her entire body a mass of sensations. Alec raised his head, his mouth seeking hers as he thrust forward one final time. She clutched at his sweat-slick shoulders as tremors buffeted her. Alec's moan of satisfaction only intensified her gratification.

She'd never felt so complete as she cradled Alec's head against the soft cushion of her breast. "Thank you, love."

His chuckle began low in his abdomen and shivered up their joined bodies. He rolled to his side without releasing her. Gently he brushed back the damp wisps of hair at her temples. "You shouldn't thank me, sweetheart. You're responsible. You're magic, my magic."

"No, we're magic together," she corrected, emboldened by the possessive look in his eyes. She lifted her head to feather a kiss across his smiling lips.

"Maybe you should get sunburn more often," Alec said, his finger lightly touching the pink of her arms. "Does it hurt?"

She blinked in surprise. She'd totally forgotten what had brought him to her bedroom. "Not at all. The aloe and something else seem to have cured me. Too bad we can't bottle it."

"Mmm, it might be a little hard to market 'Sex for sunburn' or 'Love away your pain'."

They both looked at each other expectantly and shook their heads. "Nah," they both agreed judiciously, and burst into laughter. Their amusement began to subside, but Michelle's growling stomach set them off again.

"How about dinner in bed?" he suggested when they were able to contain their laughter. "Everything's ready. You slip into that slinky yellow robe of yours, and I'll get the food."

He was up and pulling on his jeans before Michelle so much as nodded. With a wink, he strolled out the door, whistling. She lay grinning up at the ceiling. They had made love—exciting, bone-melting love. She wanted to hug the knowledge to herself and savor every moment.

THIS IS MAGIC, Michelle thought over and over again as they fed each other lobster salad and drank wine. *Laughter, love and dinner in bed by candlelight. I could definitely get used to this,* she mused, feeling utterly decadent and absolutely wonderful. She'd never felt this free with anyone. Tonight she was going to celebrate the rebirth of a fully confident Michelle Moens, and Alec Lindfors was the ideal companion to share it with.

"What would you like for dessert? Glynn left us a sherry trifle and strawberry tarts." He licked the last morsel of lobster salad from her fingers.

"You," Michelle answered, giving a husky, devilish laugh.

Alec was pleasantly surprised to discover himself under the attack of an amorous strawberry blonde. His dreams had merged into reality.

Michelle took control, sensually removing her robe in the flickering candlelight and coming to him. She cloaked their bodies in the lustrous fall of her hair while she made love to him with achingly tender slowness.

Afterward he blew out the candles, and they lay holding each other in the darkness. He knew he'd have to leave her soon before the others came home, but he waited, relishing the afterglow of their lovemaking. He wanted it to be like this always. Once they straightened out Jessica's foolishness, he would tell Michelle of his love, and they could plan a life together. Tomorrow he would begin getting everything back to normal.

HE WAS HAVING the same dream. Michelle was snuggled in his arms after a glorious night of love, her soft curves fitting perfectly against his side. Their bodies were blanketed by the thick curtain of her shimmering hair. If he opened his eyes she would disappear, and he would be alone in his room, staring up at the ceiling in frustration.

The dream changed slightly. One of Michelle's small hands was stroking his chest. She nuzzled her dainty nose into his neck, kissing the sensitive skin beneath his earlobe. Then she chuckled sleepily. That had never happened before—she'd never moved in his dream.

He snapped his eyes open. He wasn't dreaming. Michelle *was* lying next to him, snuggled contentedly against him. He had no idea of time, but maybe he could still make it to his room before the others returned. He glanced at the nightstand and groaned when he spotted Michelle's travel clock. If the time was right, he was too late, way too late. The dial read nine-fifteen. "That can't be right. I'll have to get up and check."

Reluctantly he eased himself away from Michelle. She murmured a protest, then settled back into the pillows. He scrambled into his jeans. The remains of their dinner were stacked on the tray beside the bed. Hastily he ran an eye over the room to check for evidence of his presence. Michelle didn't need his sister's knowing, triumphantly superior look to torment her. He didn't know what had made her suddenly so receptive last night, but nothing—not even his crazy sister—was going to spoil his progress.

The living room was quiet and the curtains were closed. He couldn't remember if they'd been drawn or not the night before. He headed for the kitchen to get rid of the tray and check the time on the oven clock. Just as he reached the bar he froze. Someone was turning a key in the front door. There wasn't time for him to run for cover—unless he hid behind the bar. He considered it for a minute, but dismissed the thought as ridiculous. He would stay right where he was; it was his apartment.

He regretted his decision the minute he saw the smug smile on his sister's face. His heart sank as he took in Jessica's and Philip's casual clothing. They were both in jeans and sport shirts, which meant the clock in the bedroom was right. It was after nine o'clock in the morning.

"Does this mean I get my divorce, Alec, dear?" Jessica asked sweetly. However, her simpering smile vanished at the dark look her brother shot her. "Er, how about a Danish from that fine French pastry shop, La Poule Blanche?"

"The White Hen?" Alec questioned, wondering if this wasn't still a dream, since his sister was giving the neighborhood convenience store a French name. Then he took charge. They needed to have a serious talk. He jerked his head to his right. "Into the kitchen."

He led the way and, after setting down the tray on the countertop with a decisive thud, turned to face his sister. Jessica was watching him warily, staying close to her husband. Philip, on the other hand, he noted, was having trouble containing his amusement.

"I don't want to hear any snide remarks from you, young lady," Alec snapped. "And I certainly don't want you to say a word to Michelle. Is that understood?"

"You sound exactly like Dad," Jessica complained, shifting uneasily under her brother's glare. "No, worse."

"Yeah, and I can probably find his old paddle, too. Do I make myself clear?"

"Yes, Alec," she returned meekly.

Whatever else she was going to say was cut off by the phone ringing. Alec snatched up the receiver and spoke briefly to the caller. When he'd finished he turned back to his sister. "I've got to help a friend out and play soccer. Michelle's still asleep, so leave her alone."

He didn't wait for an answer before he strolled out of the room. Though he was reluctant to leave Michelle at Jessica's mercy, he knew his love might need a breathing space. Last night had been a momentous step, and he didn't want Michelle to feel pressured. Tonight he would take her out for an elegant dinner. Alone, they could clear up both their charades.

Philip was waiting in the bedroom when Alec came out of the bathroom, straight from the shower. Alec didn't bother to speak while he pulled on his shirt and shorts.

"So, when did you discover that Jess and Michelle aren't exactly strangers?" Philip asked, grinning when his brother-in-law glanced up from tying his shoes to give him a dirty look. "I want to thank you for not strangling Jess on the spot the other night and this morning—for the baby's sake."

"Cute, Benedict, really cute. You should be thankful I didn't smother you in your sleep when I came back from the kitchen the other night. *You're* not pregnant." Alec glared at the dark-haired man. "I must be losing my touch. How did I give myself away?"

"It was just a lucky guess from your tirade in the kitchen plus umpteen years of friendship. Why else would you think Jessica might talk to Michelle about her personal life?" Philip observed, not seeming the least perturbed about the threat to his life. "Asking a woman if she's sleeping with your almost ex-husband is even too bizarre for Jess. What tipped you off to their little scam, anyway? I thought we really had you buffaloed this time."

"A very interesting picture I found in the kitchen the other night instead of a bicarb. The frame was supposedly broken the day Michelle arrived. Glynn seems to have volunteered his services to the effort."

"Let me guess. A picture under an oak tree with one of the young ladies in braids. The same one you kept on your desk at school and nearly decked Ted Hartford over when our roommate made a suggestive remark about Michelle."

"Sometimes, Benedict, you're so perceptive it scares me. However, that's why I let you marry my sister," Alec returned with a glare, resting his forearms on his thighs. "You can stay a step ahead of her, if you're not getting revenge on one of your best friends."

"I was only returning the favor of my trial by fire as a fiancé. Besides, I merely collaborated until the time seemed right to tell you what was happening. We can't let the ladies have the upper hand for too long.

"Now at the risk of severe injury, what are your intentions toward Michelle?" Philip asked without masking the steel edge to his words. "If you hurt her, I'll take you apart, or at least try to."

Alec met his old friend's level gaze, not answering immediately, but knowing the man meant every syllable. "There wouldn't be much left after I finished torturing myself. Even before I realized I was in love with her, I felt this urgent need to protect her."

"It's those big, brown eyes." Philip relaxed his rigid stance and grinned in apology. "I figured that's how it was when you laid into Jess just now, but I had to be sure. So, what happens next?"

"I'm taking Michelle out to dinner tonight, and we'll get all the deceptions out in the open." Alec hoped he sounded more confident than he felt. He was going on pure instinct that Michelle's emotions ran as deeply as his. "Once she knows I've played her along—even for a day—who knows?"

"Since I've now changed sides, I'll give you some valuable information," Philip stated with a conspiratorial look. "Michelle wanted to confess yesterday, only we persuaded her to wait a little longer."

Alec jumped to his feet and gave Philip a bone-crushing handshake, then thumped him on the back enthusiastically. He felt as though he'd received a precious gift. Now he knew Michelle felt more than just physical attraction for him.

"Hey, take it easy," Philip finally protested, flexing his abused hand. "Your sister's going to have a piece of my hide when she finds out I've switched sides, so don't batter me with happiness."

"Don't worry about Jess. I'm planning to make her squirm for this one."

"Maybe I'll join your soccer game," Philip put in hastily, eyeing Alec's satisfied smile. "Your sister can be extremely perceptive at the damnedest times. One of the hazards of marriage is mind reading."

"True, you almost blew it in the kitchen," Alec commiserated, heading for the closet. "Suit up, and let's get a move on. Revenge is sweet."

"Don't get carried away. Remember, I know my wife's future sister-in-law fairly well. *She* likes me," Philip announced with a smug smile. He was rewarded with a faceful of shirt. "I hope you propose soon. This is beginning to sound like a soap opera."

HOURS LATER Michelle gave Jessica a calculating look over the top of her menu. They'd been shopping at almost every store in Water Tower Place after a trip down the Magnificent Mile. Jessica had chatted away like an idiot one minute, then lapsed into long silences. The only time Alec's name had been mentioned was when she'd told Michelle she'd need a new dress for an evening dinner date. While Michelle was relieved she didn't have to recount the intimate details of the previous evening, she had to discover why Jessica was acting like someone who was high on diet pills. Her concern over her friend's behavior temporarily overshadowed her disappointment in missing Alec earlier.

"Fred, I slept with your brother last night," she blurted out, laying her menu on the wooden table. The restaurant was almost half-empty, giving her some privacy to get Jessica's undivided attention.

"Yes, I know," was all Jessica said as she rose halfway out of her chair to inspect the bakery shelves lining one wall.

Oh, no. She doesn't approve. Michelle frowned, but decided to forge ahead. It just didn't make sense. Jessica was the one who had bullied her into this mess, so why was she behaving this way?

"Did I tell you that Olivia is going to fix up Patrice with a soccer player she knows?" Jessica rushed into speech the minute she turned away from the pastry display. "It's really quite amusing."

"A soccer player? Now I know you're crazy. Patrice loathes professional athletes." Michelle fidgeted with her braid while Jessica gave her order to the smiling waiter who had suddenly appeared. She gave her own order in a terse voice, her impatience at fever pitch now that she'd begun. The minute the waiter's back was turned she started again. "Look at me, Jessica Wilfreda Benedict, and tell me exactly what's going on, or I'm going to stand up in this peaceful, little restaurant and scream at the top of my lungs."

Jessica's blue eyes widened in surprise, and she chewed on her lower lip. "Alec ordered me not to talk to you about last night."

"Alec ordered—" Michelle broke off in a fit of laughter, relieving her pent-up emotions. She'd never seen her friend so cowed. The thought of Alec protecting her from his own sister gave her a warm feeling underneath her amusement.

"Go ahead and laugh. Wait until he turns into an officious toad because of something *you've* done."

Michelle laughed even harder. The thought of Jessica even being the slightest bit intimidated by her brother was hysterical. She'd always assumed nothing ever stopped her friend from doing exactly what she wanted to do. Gaining some control over her amusement, she asked, "What did you do that brought on his warning?"

"I just asked if I was going to get my divorce," Jessica answered, lifting her chin defiantly as she shifted in her seat.

"And?" Michelle knew better than to take Jessica's side immediately, especially when she had that sulky look on her face.

Jessica let out a heavy sigh and answered in a singsong voice. "He was standing in the living room, holding a trayful of dirty dishes."

"Oh, Fred." Michelle knew she was grinning from ear to ear as the telltale pink of pleasure colored her cheeks. She hadn't just dreamed of sleeping all night held securely in Alec's arms.

"Since you've ruined my vow of silence, we can start planning the wedding."

"What? I think you're being a little presumptuous," Michelle said quietly, ignoring the rapid acceleration of her pulse at Jessica's words. Then she added, knowing that one of them had to be realistic. "Your brother and I are having an affair. If I can't find the problem with the computer in the next few days, I'll be going home and Comtron will send up the installation team. I've been here longer than expected as it is."

Jessica stared at Michelle, dumbfounded. Funny, squeaky noises came from her throat before she was finally able to form words. "I've created an abomination. I thought you were having doubts about a relationship with Alec, but you've got it all taken care of. I'm responsible for getting my only, beloved brother tangled up with a heartless, cruel woman. You're just going to toss poor Alec aside like dirty laundry and write things off as a good time in Chicago."

Michelle couldn't believe that Jessica was working herself into a frenzy right before her eyes. The waiter arriving with their order stopped the flow of Jessica's impassioned speech.

"Fred, I love him."

"Oh, well, that's more like it," Jessica said, and complacently took a bite of cherry croissant.

"Are you telling me you got me into this mess because you wanted to play matchmaker?"

Jessica nodded before dabbing her lips with her napkin. "Olivia's having all the fun fixing up Patrice. So I decided that if I couldn't be in Florida for the fireworks, I would dabble a little myself with the two people I love most in the entire world."

"That almost makes sense, which frightens me even more," Michelle murmured, shaking her head at the distorted logic. She sought refuge in her own chocolate-filled croissant, wondering how she was going to explain her new sense of freedom to Jessica. She was at peace over making love with Alec. There were no doubts or misgivings, and though she loved Alec, she wasn't going to force him into a commitment if he was reluctant.

"I wondered how long it would take you to figure out I wasn't really surprised about Alec's little scheme, but it was too good an opportunity to pass up," Jessica admitted with a careless shrug. "You were back in your pudgyitis funk, and although it had never occurred to me before, you and Alec are perfect together."

"Right. Alec is comfortable in any situation, urbane and charming, while I'm a blithering idiot once I leave the office," Michelle returned in total exasperation. "Fred, you definitely should consider seeking professional help."

"That's exactly my point! The two of you mesh. You learn a little self-confidence and poise from him, and he learns to care about something besides Dad's business and protecting his own feelings."

Michelle didn't have an immediate answer. She was more self-confident when she was with Alec, almost as if she drew strength from his presence. Except for the awkwardness of their first meeting, she'd always felt cherished and protected in Alec's embrace. She was also beginning to doubt the rumors about Alec's social life. If Jessica had no qualms about handing her friend over to her brother on a silver platter, then there was more smoke than fire to the newspaper accounts.

Not only did she have more self-confidence in herself, she realized, she had confidence in him, too. Tonight at dinner she would ask a few questions to erase any further misunderstandings. She promised Jessica she wouldn't confess for a few more days, but that didn't mean she couldn't find out exactly why Magda Josefsen had left Lindfors House Limited.

"You know, it's a little scary that you're the voice of sanity." Michelle gave a shaky laugh. Jessica's positive outlook was allowing her to begin hoping for the impossible. However, she was going to remain cautious. "I'm a nervous wreck, Ms Matchmaker. Are you happy?"

"Yes, as a matter of fact. You're doing an excellent job of bringing Alec back into the fold of humanity."

"Honey, if that man were any more human, I'd—" She broke off as the waiter came to collect their plate and present the check. "Your brother's not so bad."

Jessica groaned in disappointment, but immediately perked up. "Well, what's the next plan of action? That dress you tried on earlier clung in all the right places and the slight suggestion of cleavage beneath that demure lace collar will drive Alec crazy."

"Play it as it comes, Madame Machiavelli," Michelle answered as honestly as possible. She wasn't quite sure what she was going to do. Last night had been amazing, but they needed more than sexual compatibility. She was definitely done with playing games. "You're going to stay out of it this time."

"Spoilsport," the other woman complained with a resigned sigh as they gathered up their packages and left the restaurant. "That's all the thanks I get for all my help."

Michelle just shook her head as they walked to the escalator. The pitiful, little speech and Jessica's pouting lower lip didn't fool her; her friend wouldn't give up that easily. "What color are the attendants' dresses?"

Jessica turned to grin over her shoulder. "I thought a deep yellow for me as matron of honor and a tangerine shade for Patrice and Olivia."

9

"WHERE HAVE THEY disappeared to?" Alec asked his brother-in-law as he pulled two beers from the small refrigerator behind the bar. He didn't try to mask his disappointment over finding the apartment empty when they returned from the park.

"If we're lucky, a museum. If not, I'm afraid it's shop-shop-shopping," Philip answered with an exaggerated shiver of dread, taking a seat on the padded stool directly across the bar from the other man. "If I know my wife, they're now plundering Water Tower Place."

"Aren't you glad the California landscape shifts constantly to keep you in business?" Alec said with a short laugh as he handed his friend a frosty mug of imported beer. Then he leaned his elbows on the smooth teak surface of the bar, frowning after taking a healthy swallow from his mug. "How does Michelle feel about shopping?"

"Michelle's only an amateur." Philip tasted his beer and approved the brand with a nod. "However, she has a weakness for expensive lingerie."

Alec didn't make any comment. Something had been bothering him since reading Jessica's old letters. Michelle had been taken out of her shell when she was in college. She'd dated a number of men. So who or what was responsible for her extreme dislike of predatory men? He realized he could be deluding himself, but he didn't think his innocent deception alone could have made Michelle agree to Jessica's lunatic ideas.

"Why the gloomy look?" Philip prompted after a lengthy silence. "You aren't too ugly, your business is going well and you're in love with a very nice lady."

"Damning praise?"

"I try to stick to the truth whenever possible," Philip replied with a shrug. "What's bothering you?"

"Why Michelle reacted so strongly to my pretense of being married. After all, I had supposedly been separated from my wife for a number of years," Alec explained before draining the last of his beer. "I can't believe my little charade made her mad enough to go along with Jess on the spur of the moment. Or am I being a pompous ass?"

"Not this time. You're right on the money. His name was Stuart. She was involved with the clown about two or three years ago," Philip explained. "Stuart forgot to mention his wife until the lady showed up on Michelle's doorstep one day, carrying a gun."

"What?" Alec slammed down the beer bottle with which he'd been refilling their mugs. He wished the bastard who'd hurt Michelle were there in the room. A gun sounded too merciful.

"The gun wasn't loaded, but neither Michelle nor the slime knew that. Mrs. Jerk was pregnant and tired of her hubby fooling around. She sent him home at gunpoint and then cried all over Michelle." Philip paused to take a drink. Alec waited impatiently for him to continue. "It took about a year before Jess dragged the whole story out into the open. By then, Michelle had taken all the blame and crawled back into her protective shell."

"Until she took Chicago by storm," Alec interrupted with a satisfied grin. He was sure the Michelle he'd held in his arms the previous night was out of her shell.

"You know, you look damn silly with that smug grin on your face. I haven't figured it out yet, but there's something else besides Stuart that had Michelle on the war path," Philip added, gesturing with his mug for emphasis. "She didn't tell Jess about coming to Chicago in the first place, and then she called her twice after she got here."

"Undoubtedly it's the problem with my computer," Alec murmured with a frown, knowing how well developed the rumor mill was in his company. No one had liked Magda, so Michelle had probably heard more than enough.

"Problems?"

"As a result of firing an unhappy employee, I now have computer software that doesn't run quite right and a board of directors who would love to have the least, little thing go wrong with the project."

"Whoops, and Michelle's the one who has to fix it." Philip leaned his elbows on the bar and propped his chin in his hands. "I'd bet even money the former employee is a female, Nordic blonde with ice water in her veins."

"You got it in one," Alec agreed just as the phone rang. He answered, and after a brief, but pleasant conversation hung up swearing. He glared at the raven-haired man across from him as if he were responsible for his bad luck.

"Are you planning to tell me what's wrong?" Philip inquired.

"No, but I'd like to drop-kick Ted Hartford from the top floor of this building."

"Ted? He's in Saudi Arabia."

"Too true, but his brother Nathan and his wife are at the Drake," Alec grumbled. "I'm having dinner with them tonight."

"Ted's brother? Why would he be calling you?"

"Nathan's company is working on the new mall in which Lindfors House's catalog showroom will be housed. What can you do when he's a business associate and a close friend's brother?"

"I guess you change your previous reservation from two to six," Philip announced in a calm voice.

"Six?"

"Sure, Jess and I are coming along so you don't maim Nathan or make a complete idiot of yourself mooning over Michelle all night."

"You're absolutely right," Alec conceded with a regretful sigh. He couldn't believe what was happening to him. Murphy's Law had been working overtime in his life lately. There was nothing to do but talk to Michelle about everything tomorrow night.

Love wasn't supposed to be like this. Love was supposed to make you happy, Alec thought with dissatisfaction. Every time he took a step forward with Michelle, he lost two. There couldn't be anything else that would keep him from getting this mess straightened out tomorrow.

"HAIL, the conquering shoppers!" Philip heralded a half hour later as Jessica and Michelle stepped through the door. "They went, they saw, they shopped till they dropped."

"Sweetie, you know I'm shopping for two now," Jessica explained blithely, and dumped her armload of packages at his feet.

"That's a relief. You're usually shopping for about fifty," her husband returned with a jaundiced eye, assessing the purchases that littered the floor.

Michelle barely heard the couple's affectionate bickering; all her attention was centered on the silent figure behind the bar. Although she'd been anxious to see Alec every minute they were apart, she was suddenly terribly shy. He hadn't said a word since she'd arrived, but his penetrating gaze had followed her every move.

Her breath caught in her throat at the possessive hunger she saw in his eyes. Slowly he walked from behind the bar, passing his sister and brother-in-law as if they didn't exist. Michelle lowered her lashes, unable to bear his heated look. She watched his approach, mesmerized by the play of his thigh muscles below the hem of his shorts. All of a sudden he stood directly in front of her, blocking out everything else in the room.

Convulsively she tightened her arm around her packages, clutching them to her chest like a life preserver, and dared to look up. Alec's face was solemn until the moment their eyes met. A tender smile began curving his mouth, softening the planes of his face. Michelle realized he was as nervous as she was.

"Hi." Her greeting came out in a soft whisper. She gave him a tentative smile to make up for her lack of conversation. They were standing toe to toe, and she couldn't think of a single thing to say. Like a ninny, she clutched her packages in one arm and nervously twisted the fingers of her other hand around the strap of her shoulder bag.

Alec rescued her from her awkward daze, taking her hand from where she worried the strap. Holding her gaze captive, he raised her fingers to his lips. Still not saying anything, he lifted his hand to lightly trace the soft line of her cheek. His eyes told her he cherished her and that the night before had been precious to him.

A loud sigh from near the bar caused both Michelle and Alec to break their silent communication. Alec turned to the side, still holding Michelle's hand, giving her a clear view of Jessica and Philip, who weren't even trying to hide their avid interest in the scene before them. Jessica was snuggled against her husband's chest, cradled between his thighs where he sat on the bar stool. They both had an expectant look on their faces.

"Don't mind us," Jessica instructed with a broad grin.

Alec didn't bother to answer. Instead he tightened his hold on Michelle's hand and abruptly began walking toward his bedroom. She immediately dropped her packages to maintain her balance while keeping up with his long strides.

"Hey, where ya goin'? It was just getting interesting," Jessica called after the retreating pair.

"We're going where there's some privacy," Alec snarled over his shoulder as his hand closed on the doorknob. He waved Michelle through the door.

Michelle couldn't contain her laughter at Alec's harassed expression when he slammed the door behind him. He gave her a rueful shrug and then joined in her amusement. After a moment, he placed his finger to her lips to signal the need for quiet.

The light contact chased away all thoughts from Michelle's mind. She focused completely on the man in front of her; every nerve in her body attuned to him.

An infinitesimal shiver skimmed over her skin, but Alec sensed it. The lambent fire in his eyes blazed into renewed life. His admonishing touch turned to a caress, outlining the shape of her mouth.

"I've missed you, sweetheart. Every minute I was gone, I thought about coming home to you." His voice was rough with emotion, and he seemed enthralled by the pattern he drew on her lips.

"Why did you go, then?" she asked in a whisper.

"I thought you might like some time to yourself this morning," he explained with a sheepish grin. "I admit it wasn't one of my brighter ideas. I spent most of my time wanting to get back to you."

"You were being very chivalrous. I appreciate the thought, but I'd rather have woken up in your arms. Shopping with Jessica was not my first priority," she returned, finding the movement of her lips against his finger very exciting. "Not that Jessica isn't a good companion."

"We'll let Philip worry about her from now on," he instructed gently, and took a step closer. "Let's get back to the part about waking up in my arms."

Michelle trembled in earnest at the passion in his eyes. Without realizing it, she took a step backward, only to come up against the wall. He followed, placing one hand on either side of her flushed face.

"May I kiss you now, *ma belle dame*?" His husky murmur made her knees go weak. "The code of chivalry demands the lady give permission."

"*Oui, mon chevalier,*" she answered, willingly joining in his flight of fantasy.

He tasted and sipped at her mouth in brief kisses that promised but didn't satisfy. She gave a whimper of disappointment when he moved to repeat his tantalizing caress over the curve of her cheek, trailing a heated path to her temple. Softly he closed her eyes, but didn't linger, moving to her other cheek and finally back to the corner of her mouth again.

She tried to capture his lips, but Alec continued to be evasive. He controlled her movements by cradling her jaw in his large hands. Unable to withstand his taunting, she moaned his name.

"Now we know why chivalry died," he murmured against her lips, enfolding her in his embrace and burying his face in her hair. "We can't get carried away with our Peeping Toms in the living room, and we have a dinner reservation for six in about an hour and a half."

"For six?" In her surprise, she pulled back to see his face. How had their romantic evening for two become a crowd scene? The thought of the entire evening alone with Alec had shored her spirits throughout the shopping spree.

"We're having dinner with my college roommate's brother and his wife," Alec explained with a grimace, twisting a wisp of Michelle's hair around his finger. "Nathan called just after Philip and I got back. You and I were going to eat alone. You were going to be enthralled by the view of the city from the restaurant and with me."

"I think I already am," she managed, raising an unsteady finger to trace the letters on his jersey.

"Already what?" His expression was watchful, almost as if he knew her answer, but wanted the confirmation.

"I'm already enthralled with you," she responded clearly, although she couldn't meet his gaze. She continued to stare at the pattern she traced on his chest.

Alec's hand came up to capture her wandering fingers. His firm grasp carried her trembling hand to his lips and reverently he kissed her palm. "That makes two of us, *ma chère*, because I know about as much French as it takes to get through a menu and you have me spouting it like a lovesick poet."

"And very nicely, too," she assured him, finding his admission endearing. The Alec Lindfors she was discovering behind his sophisticated facade continually surprised and delighted her.

"Since we have to keep this light, would you like to hear about my aunt's pen on the desk?" he asked, and stepped back, breaking the tempting contact of their bodies.

"Hold that thought until later," she said as if he'd spoken an intimate endearment, instead of the one phrase that all beginning French students knew.

"We'll wine and dine these folks in record time, then rendezvous at our windows at eleven," he said decisively, then took a few more steps back to widen the distance between them, as though he didn't trust himself. "You go make yourself even more beautiful, if that's possible, for later tonight."

"*Jusqu'alors, mon amant brave et adroit.*" He had called her beautiful and in her confident mood, she couldn't help teasing him a little. Although how she dared calling him her skillful as well as brave lover, she didn't know. Hopefully his French really was weak, and he wouldn't ask for a full translation.

"I should demand satisfaction now, but I'll deliberate on your punishment until after dinner," he declared in a husky voice that, along with the message in his navy eyes, told Michelle she would thoroughly enjoy his retribution.

Michelle decided to retreat while she was still winning, or at least keeping even with Alec. And the faster she went to get ready for dinner, the sooner they could leave. She ran her gaze longingly over his lean body to sustain her through their brief separation, as if she were going to be miles away, instead of the width of the living room.

"It probably won't be a bad idea to tell Philip and Jessica to find a hotel for the night, either," Alec mused at the same time her hand closed around the doorknob.

His smile told her she had only seconds to get out of the room before he forgot his good intentions. Blowing him a kiss, she was out the door, and his laughter shot through her in a shiver of delight as she closed it decisively behind her.

Michelle was halfway across the living room before she remembered the presence of her two friends at the bar. In spite of the heat rising to her cheeks, she met their inquiring looks with a challenging smile. "It's a good thing curiosity isn't fatal, or both of you would be pushing up daisies. You're also going to be late for dinner if you keep playing pattycake at the bar."

She quickly retrieved her packages, thankful that the burgundy-colored chiffon of her new dress probably wasn't wrinkled from not being hung up. Alec had said he wanted her to be beautiful, and she would be. The stunned look on Jessica's and Philip's face added a spring to her step as she continued to the bedroom.

ALEC AUTOMATICALLY stood as the ladies retreated to the powder room en masse. When Michelle turned and gave him a quick wave, he wondered if he would last until eleven o'clock. He was almost tempted to follow Nathan's example in escorting his wife, Joanna. However, Michelle wasn't seven months pregnant, so someone might question his solicitousness. He simply sighed in regret as she disappeared around the foliage that separated their table from the other diners.

"I'm so glad you're enjoying our company."

Alec turned to look at his brother-in-law, not bothering to hide his irritation. "I've been sitting here, able to look but not touch for two hours. You and Nathan have been no help, discussing the joys of prospective fatherhood, giving your wives very possessive and hungry looks."

"Not touching, huh? Why is Michelle eating with only her right hand and you, your left?" Philip countered with a grin. "There was also that cozy moment that you played footsie with me, instead of Michelle."

"All right, I admit I haven't been suffering total abstinence. Let's change the subject."

"Okay, who was the distinguished gentleman who sent over the wine?" Philip asked without any complaints, his eyes were sparkling with amusement.

"Jan Josefsen, an old friend of my father's." Alec snapped out the name, not any more pleased with the new subject.

"Josefsen? That name rings a bell." Philip made a play at deep concentration. "Ahh, the ever-popular Magda."

"There's a woman who gives you nightmares. I wonder what poor sucker she's stalking now," Alec commented dryly, making it clear he really didn't care.

"Just be glad it's not you. Maybe she's found another bloodless individual like herself to have her two-point-three children with, and who'll furnish her with a shared income of over two hundred thousand a year, a house in the suburbs and good investment property in the Bahamas—as she thought you would. Did I miss anything?"

"You forgot the part about the perfect genetic match and the projection of our progeny's intelligence, not to mention the fact we would only have had to make love five times a year, during her high fertility times," Alec pointed out. For the first time since Magda had presented him with her statistical data, he was beginning to find some humor in the situation.

"Hey, it beats Jessica poking me and yelling she's ready," his brother-in-law returned with a chuckle. "I'm amazed you simply fired her. I would've contacted her family and suggested therapy."

"She's lucky I haven't contacted the police after her cute, little maneuver with the computer, but if the board got wind of the problem it would be all over," Alec stated, shaking his head at Magda's vindictive actions.

"What does Michelle know about Magda?"

"Nothing from me, but she's sure to have heard some of the rumors about my involvement with Magda. The woman didn't go quietly. If Michelle doesn't already know about the malfunction, she'll find out from me in the morning." Alec grimaced at the difficult task that lay ahead of him. "Damn Magda. She wasn't satisfied shrieking every foul name she could think of on her way out the door. She had to mess with the computer and complicate my life."

"Ouch, you have a bit of explaining to do, my friend."

"Exactly," Alec answered with a grim twist to his mouth.

"You both look like you just found out the Dow Jones dropped twenty points." Michelle's voice caused both men to start in surprise. "I hate to interrupt, but I forgot my purse."

Alec watched her closely, narrowing his eyes in speculation. How long had she been there before she'd spoken? She sounded amused but breathless, dithering slightly as she picked up her purse. With a fleeting smile, she was gone. He just might be heading for a showdown tonight instead of a romantic rendezvous. His timing was off, just as it had been ever since the moment he'd met Michelle.

Michelle fought to maintain control and not break into a run. Alec and Philip's conversation was echoing in her head. They hadn't been discussing a woman Alec had been emotionally involved with, but one who'd been an angry nuisance. Their words more than justified her growing trust in Alec's integrity. There was something else teasing her brain, as well, but she didn't have time to concentrate on it. She had to talk to Jessica. She quickly ascended the stairs to the upper level, cursing her friend's insistence that the best view was from the cocktail-lounge rest room.

Her friend was silhouetted by the glass wall that was ninety-six stories above the city, but Michelle barely paid attention. Jessica smiled in greeting as she dried her hands. "Long time, no see."

"What do you know about Magda Josefsen leaving Lindfors House?" Michelle blurted out, belatedly peeking around the corner of the stalls to make sure they were alone.

"Yuck! Why spoil a pleasant evening talking about the ice maiden?"

"Fred, this is important," Michelle continued impatiently, hoping to prevent Jessica from going off on one of her dramatic tangents. "Rumor has it that Alec fired her because their affair was over and she wouldn't leave him alone."

"About the only truth to that is that she wouldn't leave him alone."

"Fill me in, quickly," Michelle demanded. She had to make sure she'd heard the men's conversation correctly and wasn't merely interpreting it to suit herself.

Jessica detailed what she'd heard from Alec and his secretary, clearly still angry that the Josefsen woman had dared to set her sights on her brother. Most of what she said was a repetition of what Michelle already knew. "And according to Britt, the kindest thing the bloodless wonder called Alec was 'bastard.' Fortunately most of the staff was at lunch and missed her performance," Jessica concluded.

"And to get back at him, she sabotaged the computer software," Michelle murmured thoughtfully. "And I think I have a clue about how she did it."

Another woman entered the rest room, and Michelle found herself practically dragged out the door. Once Jessica had her in the corridor, she stopped.

"What's this about the computer? Alec hasn't said a word."

"It's too complicated to explain before we go back to the table. Besides, I need to mull this over," Michelle replied absently, her mind already busy turning over the solution to test it's plausibility. She smiled in triumph, wishing she could leave now to begin working it out. However, she'd just have to wait until morning and be satisfied that she had the right solution at last.

Alec sensed something different about Michelle the minute she returned to the table, and it confused him. She gave him a brilliant smile as she sat down, easing his apprehensions that she'd overheard the conversation about Magda. He relaxed over dessert, only to have his doubts return when Michelle became more and more preoccupied, remaining silent while the others argued the merits of the latest blockbuster films.

She hardly seemed to notice when Alec captured her hand under the table, his thumb intimately stroking her palm. When she did notice, her cheeks flushed a delightful pink and she ducked her head in an embarrassed apology. Her actions made Alec ever more thoughtful. He, too, withdrew from the lively conversation around them as he considered what to do next.

What could be on Michelle's mind was the basic problem. While she didn't seem to have heard the conversation about Magda, she was distracted. Without conceit, he hoped he was the cause. Perhaps she was as stunned by the suddenness of their intimacy as he was and was still trying to come to terms with it. The thought led him to a decision. He wanted all the secrets out in the open before they went any further in their personal relationship. Though an inner voice rebelled against the idea, Alec was determined. Tomorrow he would confess everything.

"Well, I don't know about you folks, but this chair isn't the most comfortable one for relaxing. Why don't we have a nightcap and coffee—or something less stimulating for the new mothers—at the apartment?" Alec tried to sound much more cheerful than he was feeling. Though the Hartfords readily accepted, he could feel three pairs of questioning eyes on him. It was small satisfaction to him that he'd finally been able to get Michelle's undivided attention for the first time in over an hour. Her puzzled look made his resolve waver slightly. He gave her hand a gentle squeeze of reassurance, knowing he was doing the right thing, even if it was the hardest moment of denial he'd ever experienced.

THE MORNING SUN streaming into the living room didn't help lighten Michelle's mood as she left the guest room. She'd had a difficult night. The possible solution to the computer glitch had warred with her confusion over Alec's strange behavior the night before. She didn't understand Alec, the genial host, who had sent her off to bed alone with no more than a chaste kiss on the forehead. His eyes had promised more, but the question was, when?

The murmur of voices from the dining area told her Glynn was back from his trip to Milwaukee and Alec had risen early. Straightening her back, she walked across the living room. She'd come to a decision about three o'clock the night before. What had seemed so rational in the dark safety of her room now had her palms sweating. The sight of Alec in a light gray suit, perfectly cut across his broad shoulders and accented by a deep mauve shirt, caused her to swallow deeply just to manage a hesitant good morning.

Alec was immediately on his feet, closing the distance between them. His gaze carried the same heated promise of the previous night. Only this morning he did something about it. He cupped her face with his hands, tilting her mouth up to meet his. Michelle luxuriated in his leisurely kiss, his tongue taunting and teasing her lower lip before delving into the moist interior of her mouth. She forgot everything but the taste and feel of him as she threaded her fingers through the silk of his hair. Being held in his arms was the perfect way to begin a day.

"Ah-hum."

The sound of Glynn clearing his throat brought Michelle back to earth. Alec ended the kiss, but didn't bother to look around, his gaze riveted to Michelle's face. She decided one of them should say something. "What is it, Glynn?"

"I was wondering if you'd like coffee, toast and juice as usual?" he asked, eyeing them with an indulgent smile. "Since you're up early, there's time for more before you leave for the office."

"The usual is fine," Michelle answered, knowing her blush was deepening, as Alec groaned. She found he was still staring at her with a hungry look.

"I don't suppose you'd consider sitting on my lap while you eat your breakfast?" he asked with a grin that brought out the single dimple in his cheek.

"Not a good idea, Mr. Lindfors," she said, attempting to give him a severe frown. Apparently whatever had come over him the night before was no longer a problem. Her heart beating double time, she took a step backward, almost surprised her legs could function. "One of us has to behave with some decorum, for Glynn's sake."

"All right, but tonight I demand as much consideration," he answered with an exaggerated sigh, somehow looking like a hurt little boy. "You sit down, and I'll pick up your belongings."

Michelle took a step toward her chair, then stopped to look over her shoulder. Alec was picking up her jade-green suit jacket, her briefcase and her purse. She realized she'd dropped them sometime during his warm greeting.

The minute she sat down Glynn appeared with the coffeepot and her breakfast. She counted under her breath to steady her nerves as the ever-efficient Glynn poured her coffee and added just the right amount of Worcestershire sauce to her tomato juice.

"Alec." She'd managed to say his name at the same time he said "Michelle." Both of them stopped with a nervous laugh, then Alec gestured for her to go ahead.

"I just wanted to let you know that I think I've come up with the solution to the software problem." She cringed inwardly at the awkward statement, but pressed on. "Now don't be too optimistic, because I'm working on a hunch. However, I think Lew and I will be able to work out Magda's passwording system and have everything back to normal by tomorrow."

Her recitation done, she sat primly with her hands folded on the edge of the table and she waited for Alec to answer. When he didn't say a word, she glanced to the side. He was watching her with narrowed eyes, as if to determine what she was thinking.

She couldn't bear the silence, so she decided to continue, hoping Alec would respond to something, anything. "Lew said that the board meeting was sometime this week and that we needed to have a report ready by then. Well, you can see that it's difficult to write a report with software that doesn't work. I didn't think you'd want the board to have a gloomy projection of the costs of reinstalling a new program or wonder why Lew and I weren't clever enough to outthink a discontented employee. If this hunch of mine—"

"Michelle, stop," Alec broke in, a dazed look on his face. Tilting his head, he gave a ghost of a smile. "How long do you think you could have kept up the prattle?"

"Not much longer," she admitted, giving him a sheepish grin. Unlacing her fingers, which had become stiff from being clenched, she reached for her juice. Things were going fairly well; Alec was taking her explanation very calmly.

What do I do next? Alec thought wildly. He was torn between slinking under the table or jumping up to rain kisses all over Michelle's flushed face. He knew he could do neither, though the latter was very tempting. The lady always managed to surprise him, getting one step ahead of him on unraveling the layers of their deceptions. Her matter-of-fact talk about Magda was a positive sign, one he hadn't thought would materialize so effortlessly.

"Michelle Moens, have I told you lately that you're wonderful?" he said, not quite keeping the huskiness out of his voice. "You're a lady with beauty, brains and the sweetest kisses on earth."

He watched her nervously turn her wheat toast into crumbs, a vivid blush rising from the draped collar of her oyster-colored blouse to the roots of her tousled hair. "We have a lot to discuss tonight," he continued, reaching across the table to capture her chin between his thumb and forefinger. He wanted to see her beautiful brown eyes. "Tonight I promise that we'll be alone. We'll talk about us and the future. Nothing is going to keep us apart from now on. Go fix your hair and lipstick before I decide that I couldn't care less about my board of directors, computer problem or bad-tempered ex-employees. Soon I'll be taking the pins from your hair without a thought to Glynn or decorum."

"I'll meet you at the elevator in a few minutes," she said, getting up as she spoke. She took a few steps, then turned slightly, giving him a challenging smile. "I'm going because I want this stupid computer problem out of the way. In the future, you're going to to have to give me a less tempting choice than work or you. *You* are going to win every time."

Alec slumped in his chair as she disappeared around the corner. Was tonight going to be this easy? He rubbed the back of his neck as he considered what needed to be thrashed out. If Michelle was this reasonable about Magda, then his admitting to having known about the scheme she and Jessica had cooked up shouldn't be too difficult. With a sigh, he wondered why facing Hauser and the rest of the board was beginning to look like the easier prospect.

10

"TRUST ME, LEW. I know what an angry woman could do," she told the younger man two hours later after going over the printouts of the failed attempts to break Magda's coding. His incredulous look while reading her list of possible passwords and listening to her theory told Michelle she would have an uphill battle. "Women don't use 'gosh darn' or 'shuckie dern' to express their feelings when they're furious."

"Yeah, but Magda had icicles for feelings and was *mucho* smart," Lew replied, scratching his head and pushing his glasses back into place with his index fingers. "She just isn't the type."

"I'm the type, so why not her? Besides, she didn't have time for something too complex, *and* she was furious, already spouting foul names."

"Oooookay," he agreed, but he still looked skeptical.

She bit her lip, feeling some remorse at destroying his naive belief that women were perfect. In the next half hour, she forgot her misgivings as Lew began thinking up words of his own. He even blushed beet red when he muttered what he called "the big one." Things got slightly out of hand and nothing was accomplished for a while as they laughed and tried to top each other with outrageous suggestions. Weak with laughter and holding each other upright, neither of them saw Alec enter the computer room, then leave as silently as he had come.

Once they had settled down to the task, the work was tedious. Both of them reminded each other of the cardinal rule of programming—if it's estimated to take half an hour, then schedule eight. Almost immediately they succeeded with the word *bastard*, but Magda had been very thorough, using layers of passwords. They managed to work their way through four layers by five o'clock. At that point, they knew they needed a break.

When Michelle called the apartment and didn't get an answer, she decided to make a quick trip to change clothes and leave Alec a note. She and Lew returned to the program with renewed energy after an hour's break. By eight o'clock they'd cracked the fifth and final layer. For good measure, Lew ran part of the accounts backlog through the computer.

After a brief victory polka around the computer room, Michelle collapsed in the chair behind Lew's desk, a satisfied smile on her face. Now she could go home to Alec with the good news, and no matter what promises she'd made Jessica, she was going to tell him everything. Savoring her victory, she waved Lew off to go share the rest of the evening with his girlfriend. She leaned her head back on the soft padding of the chair, rocking gently as she thought of the delights ahead in Alec's arms. The blinking light on the telephone went unnoticed as she drifted into a much-needed sleep.

HOURS LATER, Michelle didn't bother to stifle her jaw-popping yawn as she nodded at the apartment security guard and entered the elevator. She was still furious with herself for falling asleep, wasting precious hours that could have been spent with Alec.

The apartment was silent as she let herself in quietly. The living room curtains were open, drawing her to the panorama of the city lights. She looked out, rubbing the back of her neck to relax her stiff muscles, wondering what to do next. Did she peek in each bedroom like Goldilocks, to see where she was sleeping tonight? She still didn't have an answer as she stretched with her fingers interlaced, pushing her arms above her head.

"Well, well, well, what do we have here?" Alec's bitter voice stopped her with her arms still stretched in the air. "Why, if it isn't Ms Michelle Moens. Or should I call you 'Hal'?"

He was standing in front of the planked table in the dining area, not a foot from where he'd kissed her that morning. Leaning back against the table, he crossed his arms over his chest. His fair hair gleamed in the moonlight; it was mussed, as if he'd been running his fingers through it continually. He was still dressed in the clothes he'd worn to work. The gray pants now needed pressing, and his shirt was unbuttoned halfway down his chest just above the loosened knot of his striped tie.

What kept Michelle from uttering a word was the haunted look on his face, half-hidden in the shadows. His eyes bored into hers with bleak anger. He'd called her "Hal," so she knew where the anger came from: Alec knew she was Jessica's friend.

"I'm so glad you've decided to grace us with your presence once again," he continued when she remained silent, her only movement the lowering of her arms when she turned to face him. "To what do we owe this great honor?"

"Alec, I'm sorry. I didn't want you to find out this way." She moved forward slowly. Alec was holding himself in tight control, only his voice showing his emotions. "Believe me—"

His harsh laugh was a sound Michelle hoped she'd never hear again. "Believe you? Isn't that rich. You say you're working, but no one's at the office. Did you suddenly discover you prefer a younger man? Is his IQ going to compensate for his inexperience in bed?"

What is the man talking about? Michelle began to wonder if she was still sleeping in Lew's office. She decided to take one thing at a time. One, Alec knew her nickname. Two, he was extremely angry. Three, he was accusing her of being out with a younger man. Lew? Surely he couldn't think she wanted to be with Lew and not with him. She wanted to laugh and put her arms around him at the ludicrous idea. The gorgeous, self-assured Alec Lindfors was jealous over her. Amazing.

"You certainly had everyone fooled with your shy, innocent doe-brown eyes. That sweet, pristine Gibson girl facade gives the impression you need protection," Alec said, continuing his tirade. He kept his eyes on her face as she walked toward him. "You need about as much protection as a she wolf guarding her young. And what really galls me is my own sister defending you. Even Glynn is on your side."

"Alec, I have to tell you about the computer," Michelle said softly, hoping to break into his irrational babbling.

"That damn computer. I wish I'd never had the bright idea to automate. Then I'd never have met you." He almost snarled when she stopped in front of him. "A woman who can't even come up with a convincing lie. So, tell me about working on the computer all night. Was it so engrossing that you couldn't answer the phone when I called—five times?"

"I have been working on your blasted computer, and it's working beautifully," she returned, raising her voice. It seemed to be the only way to get his attention. "I don't know anything about phone calls. If you were so concerned, why didn't you come to the office?"

The question hung in the air between them as Alec snapped his mouth shut, abruptly cutting off whatever blistering words he was going to say. He blinked at her like a startled owl, and she savored the moment. Although she was beginning to understand his anger, she felt some pleasure at having dumbfounded him.

"Now that I have your attention, I'll tell you what happened. Lew and I finally broke through Magda's security program about eight o'clock and we ran a sample of the accounts program, which worked perfectly," she explained in a slow steady voice, making sure he heard every word. "Unfortunately I relaxed a little too soon and fell asleep in Lew's office after he left. One of the security guards woke me up during his rounds, or I'd probably still be there."

Alec couldn't believe what a total ass he'd just made of himself. When his calls to Lindfors House had gone unanswered all he could think about was how easily Michelle laughed around Lew and the cozy little scene he'd interrupted in Lew's office when the younger man had been rubbing her shoulders. The longer Michelle was away, the more he'd fretted about where she was and whom she was with.

After all, he'd reasoned, he was approaching forty, and any day now his hair would start receding. Michelle wasn't that much older than Lew, and they did have a number of things in common. After his fifth unsuccessful call, he began blaming Michelle. She was a devious woman who'd been fooling all of them.

"Alec, aren't you going to say anything about my friendship with Jessica?"

Still reliving his nightmarish evening, he answered absently, "Oh, I've known about Jessica's scheme since the night she and Philip arrived."

"You knew?" Michelle's pointed question drew him out of his thoughtful daze. He understood immediately that he should have told her more diplomatically. Even in the moonlight he could see that her brown eyes had narrowed in speculation and her shoulders were rigid. He should have waited until they were both calmer, but after waiting so long to clear up their deceptions, he'd wanted it done with.

"You stood there ranting about my running out on you with a younger man, and the whole time you've been laughing at me?" Her voice started in a low, accusing tone but was quickly a hysterical pitch. Although tears glistened in her eyes, her hands were on her hips in a militant pose.

"Michelle, please. I didn't laugh at you. I was flattered." He smiled and reached for her as he explained.

Michelle wasn't ready to be reasonable. She slapped away his hand from where it rested on her shoulder. "Flattered? You were flattered? And should I be overjoyed that I pleased the oh-so-sought-after Alec Lindfors, who has so many women he has to lie about being married to keep away the droves of admirers. I just spent the day, and night, cleaning up after one of your women. How nice I flattered you."

"This is ridiculous, sweetheart. There isn't any reason for us to be fighting," Alec replied in his most coaxing voice, with a gentle smile for good measure.

"Don't flash that silly dimple at me, buster. I just spent over twelve hours working on that damn computer. For what?" She raised one hand and gestured in the air to emphasize her point, even though it didn't make sense. "Magda Josefsen was right. You are a bastard."

She turned in an abrupt about-face and walked on stiff legs to the middle of the living room. Then she remembered she didn't know which room was vacant. Rather than admit her dilemma, she vented her frustration by turning to Alec. "I could just beat myself for feeling sorry for you and for being understanding. I believed your sister and your friends when they said I was helping you be more human. Now I know why you backed off suddenly—you were tired of the game."

"Look, honey, why don't we talk about this later after we've gotten some sleep."

"After I get some sleep, I'm going back to Atlanta on the first flight out of O'Hare, Mr. Scandinavian Stud, so don't suggest we get some sleep together," she snapped, her temper showing no sign of abating. "The next time you need a rep from Comtron, I'll recommend they send a robot. The two of you will have a lot in common, and it won't have any feelings for you to trample over."

"In that case, I guess this is goodbye," Alec returned, feeling his own anger coming back. She was pigheaded, hot tempered and gorgeous. He narrowed the distance between them in quick strides. Before Michelle could utter a word of protest, he took her in his arms.

She parted her lips to object, and Alec took full advantage. He drew out the kiss, willing her to soften in his embrace. Michelle resisted the full **arsenal of** his skill as he tasted and cajoled, seeking some response. A telltale tremor was the only sign of the chaotic emotions urging her to give in to the molten fire he was creating.

"Sweet dreams, love," he murmured when he released her and stepped back. "I'll join the others at the house in Lake Forest. For some reason, they thought we might want to be alone. Have a safe trip home."

As he walked away Alec wondered if he was convincing. He was gambling. If he left her alone now, they could make up in the morning before Michelle had a chance to pack. He wasn't about to let her walk out of his life.

She wasn't going to let him have the last word, Michelle decided as she watched him walk away with what she thought was a definite swagger. "Maybe I will try a younger man, after all, Mr. Lindfors. They say 'get 'em young and teach 'em,' don't they? I certainly hope a younger man wouldn't fall asleep from too much wine while he's making love to me."

Alec swung around abruptly, his expression masked in the darkness. He didn't say a word. Michelle braced herself for what was to come. However, he turned away without a word, which was worse than anything he could have said.

She dropped into the nearest chair the minute the hall door closed behind him. That was a cheap shot, she knew, but it was no more damaging than his casual statement that he'd known her identity for days. For a moment she allowed her trembling body to react to the soul-shattering kiss that had just taken place, even though she knew she didn't have the luxury. Alec would be back sooner than he thought. She had to be safely in her room when he remembered he didn't have any shoes on.

Though she was exhausted after a day of outwitting Magda Josefsen and arguing with Alec, she was still awake an hour later and staring up at the ceiling. Alec hadn't returned. Apparently he was angry enough to overlook his need for shoes. Tossing back the sheet, she gave in to an impulse. She padded across the living room and, in spite of cautious thought, climbed into Alec's bed and snuggled under the covers, telling herself all the while that this was what had gotten her into trouble in the first place.

As she drifted into sleep all she could think about was Alec's admission that he'd known who she was. Had she played the fool because of a man again? Just when she thought she could believe in the man's integrity, she was uncertain. But not as uncertain as Alec had been when she hadn't come back to the apartment on time, she remembered with a dreamy smile. Perhaps she wouldn't call the airport the minute she woke up in the morning. Or perhaps she'd go back to Atlanta and take a chance Alec cared enough to come after her. She didn't stay awake long enough to make a choice.

ALEC LET HIMSELF back into the apartment an hour later, wondering what kind of reception he would receive. He fingered his keys nervously as if they were worry beads. He'd gotten over halfway to Lake Forest before he decided he was being an idiot. Michelle was alone in his apartment and he was leaving her to go stay with the three people who had been underfoot for days. When he realized what he was doing, he turned swiftly back.

Now all he had to do was get himself back in her good graces. Though he was still stinging from her trick of leaving him on the couch, he was beginning to see the humor of it—just. All that was past history, anyway. They needed to start, or at least go on, as themselves without any pretenses.

"Well, you aren't going to get anywhere out here, Lindfors." Even his little pep talk lacked confidence. It amazed him how petrified he was that something else would go wrong. "It's now or never."

He crossed to the guest room in three strides, stopping only when he realized the door was standing open. She couldn't have gone already, could she? A shiver of cold fear raced down his spine at the thought. He bounded into the room, appalled when he saw the bed empty. Still doubtful, he snapped on the bedside light and began searching the room. It only took a minute to discover that her clothes were still there.

Alec stood absolutely still in the middle of the room, a slight smile beginning to form as he considered where she could be. He was almost afraid to go see if it was true. He ambled out of the room and across the living room, pausing at the door to his own room. Then he opened the door silently and stepped into total darkness. When his eyes adjusted to the absence of light, he saw her. She was lying on her side, her arms wrapped around one of the pillows. She was right where she belonged, in his bed.

He shook his head as he savored the moment. This time she was in his bed by choice, not through his wily manservant's machinations. But how could she sleep at a time like this. Of course, she'd slept all night in his arms once without being aware of it, he reasoned. Why shouldn't she wake up in his arms again? He needed to hold her.

Before he could reconsider, he carefully emptied his pockets and took off his clothes. Michelle didn't stir even when he climbed in beside her.

Cautiously he pulled the pillow out of her arms and gently placed her head on his shoulder. She snuggled her face into the curve of his neck as if she did it every night. Her arms came to rest on his shoulders. Alec wasn't sure he'd made the right decision. Though Michelle didn't know he was there, he was all too aware of the soft curves he cradled in his arms. He was headed for a night of exquisite torture. Just holding her and inhaling her perfume was arousing him.

He couldn't resist stroking her hair. She moved restlessly under his caress, one hand tangling in the springy hair of his chest. "Alec?"

"It'd better not be anyone else," he growled, tightening his arms around her waist.

"If I open my eyes, will you still be here?" Her voice was husky with sleep, and tentative, as if she really were afraid he was a fantasy.

"Yes, sweetheart, I'll be here even if I turn on the light," he assured her, chuckling over her question. He felt better than he had all day. She wasn't going to throw him out.

"Would you?"

"Would I what, love?"

"Turn on the light. I want to see you," she said, her voice stronger now that she was waking up.

He complied with her request, but kept one arm around her. He, too, needed proof she was there.

She blinked up at him as her eyes adjusted to the sudden light. "What took you so long?"

She had to keep from laughing out loud at the stunned look on his face. She watched in fascination as the wariness left his eyes and was replaced by amusement. His hand came up to cup her cheek.

"I'm not letting you out of my sight again, and you're going to tell me exactly what you're doing every minute of the day," he stated firmly, his eyes never leaving her face.

"Sort of takes the mystery out of a relationship, doesn't it?" She couldn't resist teasing him now that he was holding her in his arms. His presence filled her with confidence, so it was hard to contain her happiness.

"Sweetheart, I think we've had enough intrigue to last us for a while," he answered, beginning to grin at her antics. "We'll let Glynn dabble in conspiracies—which won't include putting eligible young ladies in bed just because he thinks it will be good for me."

"You meant it wasn't an accident?" Michelle giggled at the thought of staid Glynn manipulating them even more than Jessica.

"Yes, he confessed earlier to help calm me down after I couldn't get you on the phone," Alec explained with a frown. "If we can control my sister and him, we should be able to settle down as a nice, normal couple from now on."

"Sounds boring to me," Michelle replied quickly. She laid her hand on his chest and rested her chin on it as she stuck out her lower lip in a pout of discontentment."

"Nothing is boring when you're in love." Alec's face was serious as he said the words, a catch in his voice.

"Then we shouldn't be bored for a very, very long time." She could see he needed her reassurance. A wave of tenderness washed over her at the thought of his need for her, a need strong enough to bring him back to her tonight, but she needed to hear the words. "Say it, please?"

"I love you, Michelle Moens. I love you in your prim business suits and track shoes. I love you when you're seducing me and when you're teasing me." He leaned forward, emphasizing each declaration with a kiss. Beginning at her forehead, he gradually worked his way down to hover over her lips. "Now it's your turn."

"You beast," she whispered without any real threat. Before she gave in to his request, she was going to taste his kiss. Her fingers tangled in his hair to keep him from pulling back. First she outlined the chiseled shape of his mouth with her tongue, teasing and arousing him. He tried to deepen the kiss, but she wouldn't let him. Still taking her time, she nibbled at his lips until he groaned in frustration. Unable to resist any longer, she gave him the kiss they were both longing for.

Alec took control at once, turning her in his arms until she was lying on her back. His body pressed hers into the mattress, but he didn't continue the kiss.

"Now what did you want to tell me? I won't make love to a woman who doesn't love me," he growled, and dipped his head to rain butterfly kisses along her arched neck.

"I love you, Alec Lindfors. I love you when you're bossy in your expensive suits. I love you when you're seducing me and telling me outrageous fibs." She stopped to take a deep breath, reveling in their teasing foreplay. His hands were moving over the silk of her nightgown, setting her body on fire. "I even love you when you speak wretched French."

"You beautiful witch," he accused with a tolerant chuckle. "We'll make a pact. I won't ever speak French again, except to order food, and you take off this ridiculous piece of fluff that's keeping me from your luscious body."

"Darling, all you had to do was ask." She giggled at his fierce scowl and raised her arms over her head in invitation.

Alec didn't wait. He sat up and threw back the sheet. Michelle was surprised when he didn't rip the material from her, even though his eyes told her that was what he'd like to do. He skimmed his hands down her body from her shoulders, lingering over her breasts before traveling downward to the lace hem of her nightgown. Then he slipped his hands under the material, splaying his fingers to pull it taut, before retracing his caress.

Michelle arched her back to allow him to remove the nightgown. She couldn't hold back her moan of approval when his lips began moving over her collarbone. Slowly, teasingly, his lips caressed her breasts, brushing over but never settling on the hardened peaks. His hands moved more rapidly to untie the tiny bows that held her bikini briefs together. Without the silken barrier his fingers found the dewy moisture of her femininity.

"Alec, please love me," she pleaded when his lips glided over the sensitive skin of her abdomen.

"I am, my love. I am," he replied, not raising his head.

She tangled her fingers in his tousled hair to stop him. "Now, darling. I want you inside me. Don't wait."

Her desire-clouded voice made him look up. She begged him with her eyes to take her, showing him how much she needed him.

He rose above her, parting her legs. Both of them cried out in satisfaction when he entered her in one fluid motion. Alec began a slow rhythm that Michelle was quick to accompany. When he didn't increase the pace, she wrapped her legs around his lean hips, forcing him to move faster. Their lips came together in a searing kiss, their tongues dueling for domination.

Neither of them could hold back. They expressed their love and need with their bodies. All too soon they reached the ultimate summit of pleasure.

Michelle cradled Alec's spent body in her arms. She wanted to laugh and cry at the beauty of the moment. A single tear slid down her cheek, and Alec pulled back to look at her face.

"You're crying, love," he said in a worried whisper, capturing the droplet with his finger.

"With happiness, you beautiful man," she murmured in return, and reached up to trace the lips that gave her such pleasure.

"Are you going to marry me?" He rolled onto his side, closing his hands around her wandering fingers. While he waited for her answer, he kissed the tip of each one.

"Yes, you arrogant man, I'll marry you in three months," she stated firmly, and kissed him to seal her promise, smiling up at his imperiously raised eyebrows. "I knew your self-confidence would return all too soon."

Alec ignored her comment for the more important matter. "Three months? I wish we'd met years ago, so we could be celebrating at least our tenth anniversary by now." His voice was wistful, and she knew she'd better clarify her reason for the delay quickly.

"If we'd met then, I would have run away and hid. You would have scared me to death," she said with a self-deprecating laugh. "I was still jumping at shadows in those days."

"Is that why you want to wait three months?" Alec broke in anxiously. "You're not sure?"

"Don't look so worried, darling. I'm very sure, but I'm being realistic," she answered, smoothing his damp hair away from his temple. "I have to give notice, find out where we're going to live—"

"Oh, God, you haven't seen the house," he exclaimed as her meaning sank in.

"I saw it years ago, but we do need some time together," Michelle reminded him with an indulgent smile.

"I'm beginning to wish for just a little of the hesitancy you had when you first arrived. Maybe I was wrong in assuming you were a dupe in my crazy sister's plot." He sighed regretfully, turning soulful eyes to meet her laughing gaze.

"I must have seemed like a tasty morsel for a tiger on the prowl, if that's how I looked to you." She pretended to pout again, but couldn't maintain the pose. "Our love is what's responsible for all this newfound confidence, my love. You've given me the strength to believe in myself."

Alec's eyes had a sheen of moisture after her declaration. "You said you were making me human again, and you were right. I've never felt so humble or undeserving in my life."

"I've always known you were human. That's been my problem from the start. You are a very human, sexy and irresistible man," she stated with conviction, and stroked him with a loving hand. "And also very virile. You don't know how hard it was to leave you on the couch that night."

"I haven't quite forgiven you for that yet," he growled. He bent his head to give her a punishing kiss. "Promise me you'll never do that again."

"We'll both promise never to play practical jokes on each other. We'll work together to plot against your sister," Michelle pledged, returning his kiss with a tantalizing caress that promised more excitement. "I have one last request before you have permission to ravage my lily-white body."

"That kind of favor will grant any request, my tigress," he assured her, beginning to stroke her receptive body before she formed her question.

"Promise me that the newspapers understand there's only one Mrs. Alec Lindfors," she murmured in his ear. "And that she's very jealous, like her husband, and doesn't take kindly to having her husband's picture taken with anyone else but his wife."

"That will be easy, sweetheart, because after today's harrowing experience, I don't plan to let you go any farther than a foot from my side," Alec stated determinedly. "That will be true for the next fifty or sixty years."

"As Glynn would say, that's just as it should be," Michelle agreed, then expressed one, last rational thought before giving herself up to the magic of Alec's embrace. "I really think you should give Glynn a raise for our first night together."

HARLEQUIN *Temptation*

COMING NEXT MONTH

#265 SECOND TO NONE Rita Clay Estrada

Brad Bartholomew's father and Gina O'Con's mother had shared a deep and forbidden love for twenty years. As if destined to recreate their passion, Brad and Gina were inexorably drawn to each other, even though the past might stand between them....

#266 MACNAMARA AND HALL Elise Title

When next-door-neighbors Tracy Hall and Tom Macnamara got together to coach their kids' little league team, they quickly discovered they were a hit *off* the diamond, too. In fact, it was clear from the outset that Tom and Tracy's love was heading for the big leagues!

#267 BEST-LAID PLANS Mary Tate Engels

Mayor Lacy Donahue had a winning strategy for revitalizing Silverton, New Mexico: Holt Henderson. Holt's talent at restoration could change the face of the small mining town. But Holt's devastating appeal could topple Lucy's reserve. And that was something her honor hadn't planned on.

#268 CODE NAME: CASANOVA
Dawn Carroll

Agent Daniel Avanti was the most charming devil who had ever walked the earth. Kerith Anders was his last assignment before he retired the code name Casanova.

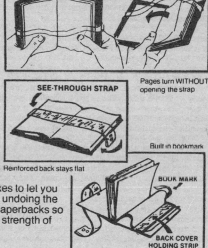

SWEEPSTAKES RULES & REGULATIONS

NO PURCHASE NECESSARY TO ENTER OR RECEIVE A PRIZE

1. To enter and join the Reader Service, check off the "YES" box on your Sweepstakes Entry Form and return to Harlequin Reader Service. If you do not wish to join the Reader Service but wish to enter the Sweepstakes only, check off the "NO" box on your Sweepstakes Entry Form. Incomplete and/or inaccurate entries are ineligible for that section or sections(s) of prizes. Not responsible for mutilated or unreadable entries or inadvertent printing errors. Mechanically reproduced entries are null and void. Be sure to also qualify for the Bonus Sweepstakes. See rule #3 on how to enter

2. Either way, your unique Sweepstakes number will be compared against the list of winning numbers generated at random by the computer. In the event that all prizes are not claimed, random drawings will be held from all entries received from all presentations to award all unclaimed prizes. All cash prizes are payable in U.S. funds. This is in addition to any free, surprise or mystery gifts that might be offered. The following prizes are offered: *Grand Prize (1) $1,000,000 Annuity; First Prize (1) $35,000; Second Prize (1) $10,000; Third Prize (3) $5,000; Fourth Prize (10) $1,000; Fifth Prize (25) $500; Sixth Prize (5,000) $5.

   * This Sweepstakes contains a Grand Prize offering of a $1,000,000 annuity. Winner may elect to receive $25,000 a year for 40 years without interest; totalling $1,000,000 or $350,000 in one cash payment. Entrants may cancel Reader Service at any time without cost or obligation to buy.

3. Extra Bonus Prize: This presentation offers two extra bonus prizes valued at $30,000 each to be awarded in a random drawing from all entries received. To qualify, scratch off the silver on your Lucky Keys. If the registration numbers match, you are eligible for the prize offering.

4. Versions of this Sweepstakes with different graphics will be offered in other mailings or at retail outlets by Torstar Corp. and its affiliates. This promotion is being conducted under the supervision of Marden-Kane, Inc., an independent judging organization. By entering this Sweepstakes, each entrant accepts and agrees to be bound by these rules and the decisions of the judges, which shall be final and binding. Odds of winning in the random drawing are dependent upon the total number of entries received. Taxes, if any, are the sole responsibility of the winners. Prizes are nontransferable. All entries must be received by March 31, 1990. The drawing will take place on or about April 30, 1990 at the offices of Marden-Kane, Inc., Lake Success, N.Y.

5. This offer is open to residents of the U.S., United Kingdom and Canada, 18 years or older, except employees of Torstar Corp., its affiliates, subsidiaries, Marden-Kane and all other agencies and persons connected with conducting this Sweepstakes. All Federal, State and local laws apply. Void wherever prohibited or restricted by law.

6. Winners will be notified by mail and may be required to execute an affidavit of eligibility and release, which must be returned within 14 days after notification. Canadian winners will be required to answer a skill-testing question. Winners consent to the use of their name, photograph and/or likeness for advertising and publicity in conjunction with this or similar promotions, without additional compensation.

7. For a list of our most current major prize winners, send a stamped, self-addressed envelope to: Winners List, c/o Marden-Kane, Inc., P.O. Box 701, Sayreville, N.J. 08871

If Sweepstakes entry form is missing, please print your name and address on a 3" × 5" piece of plain paper and send to:

In the U.S.	In Canada
Sweepstakes Entry	Sweepstakes Entry
901 Fuhrmann Blvd.	P.O. Box 609
P.O. Box 1867	Fort Erie, Ontario
Buffalo, NY 14269-1867	L2A 5X3